"Quent Yerby, Don't You Dare Leave Like This."

He cocked his head and gave Beck a sidelong glance. She looked gorgeous. Her long, black hair was disheveled from his loving, her cheeks rosy and her lips swollen from his passion. "Don't worry, sweet thing...I'll be back tomorrow to get you and my nephew."

"What?"

"My place is small, but we can make do with one bedroom. Josh can bunk with me, and you can take the couch."

"One bedroom? Sleep on the couch? No!"

Quent walked toward his car, then turned around. Beck glared at him.

"Try to be ready by noon," he said. "I don't like to be kept waiting."

Beck slammed the front door. Damn obnoxious, overbearing male chauvinist, redneck...

What was she going to do? She had no doubt Quent could and would protect her and Josh from the man who stalked them. But who was going to protect her from Quent Yerby?

Dear Reader,

Welcome to Silhouette Desire! If this is your first Desire novel, I hope it will be the first of many. If you're a regular reader, you already know that you're in for a treat.

Every Silhouette Desire book contains a romance to remember. These stories can be dramatic or humorous... topical or traditional. Each and every one is a love story that is guaranteed to sweep you into a world of passion. The heroines are women with hopes and fears just like yours. And the heroes—watch out! You won't want to read about just one. It will take all six of these strong men to keep you satisfied.

Next month, look for a special treat... six tantalizing heroes you'll want to get to know—and love—in *Men of the World*. These sinfully sexy men are from six different and romantic countries. Each book has the portrait of your hero on the cover, so you won't be able to miss this handsome lineup. Our featured authors are some of the finest: BJ James, Barbara Faith, Jennifer Greene, Lucy Gordon, Kathleen Korbel and Linda Lael Miller. *Men of the World*—don't miss them.

And don't miss September's *Man of the Month* book, *Lone Wolf* by Annette Broadrick. It sizzles!

Happy reading,

Lucia Macro
Senior Editor

BEVERLY BARTON

OUT OF DANGER

SILHOUETTE *Desire*®

Published by Silhouette Books New York

America's Publisher of Contemporary Romance

SILHOUETTE BOOKS
300 East 42nd St., New York, N.Y. 10017

OUT OF DANGER

ISBN: 0-373-05662-1

First Silhouette Books printing September 1991

Books by Beverly Barton

Silhouette Desire

Yankee Lover #580
Lucky in Love #628
Out of Danger #662

BEVERLY BARTON

has been in love with romance since her grandfather gave her an illustrated book of *Beauty and the Beast*. An avid reader since childhood, she began writing at the age of nine and wrote short stories, poetry, plays and novels through high school and college. After marriage to her own "hero" and the births of her daughter and son, she chose to be a full-time home-maker, a.k.a. wife, mother, friend and volunteer.

Six years ago, she began substitute teaching and returned to writing as a hobby. In 1987, she joined the RWA and soon afterward helped found the Heart of Dixie chapter in Alabama. Her hobby became an obsession as she devoted more and more time to improving her skills as a writer. Now her lifelong dream of being published has come true.

To my support group friends, who have shared with me their love for and knowledge of writing: Patricia Rorie, Willie Wood, Edna Waits and Sheila Hargett.

Special thanks to: Jane and Johnny Harrison, for being my wonderful Memphis tour guides, and Ed Woodward, for introducing me to "Cool Jazz."

Prologue

The front door of Beck's town house stood wide open. Clutching the bag of groceries in her arms, she ran toward her apartment. She entered the small foyer, then stopped short and listened.

"Jill?" After a moment of silence, she called again, "Jill?" It was past six, and she knew that both Jill and Jill's son, Josh, should be home.

Suddenly Beck heard soft, hurt cries. Bracing herself for whatever she might find, she walked into the living room. Nothing looked out of place. The room appeared to be as neat and tidy as when she'd left this morning. Then she heard the incoherent cries again. They came from behind the sleek sectional sofa.

She moved quickly, praying with each step... and then gasped at the sight of the woman lying crumpled on the thick tan carpet.

Jill's slender body lay sideways, curled in a fetal position, her arms clutching her stomach. A rangy, shaggy-haired man knelt over her, his fist drawn back, ready to strike. He turned his head at the sound of Beck's indrawn breath. Demonic eyes stared at her.

Beck couldn't move. Her heart pounded wildly and her stomach quivered as her head filled with a rush of adrenaline. She swayed, ever so slightly.

Without warning, the man stood up and walked toward her. Beck began backing out of the living room, intending to run. He reached out for her. Dropping the paper bag, she grabbed a wooden sculpture off a nearby table and threw it at the attacker. The heavy art piece hit the man on the shoulder, slowing his movements long enough for Beck to escape into the foyer. Just as he caught up with her at the open front door, Beck let out a bloodcurdling scream.

Obviously stunned, the man burst through the door, knocking her aside. His dark, glazed eyes met hers briefly as he hurtled past her.

Beck's body shook. She took deep, cleansing breaths before abruptly turning to go back inside the town house.

Filled with dread, she ran into the living room and fell to her knees beside her young friend. "Dear God, Jill."

"Royce," Jill whispered. "He... he found... us." Each word escaped from her lips on a tortured sigh.

With trembling hands, Beck touched Jill's battered face, her beautiful face now almost unrecognizable. Fresh blood stuck to Beck's fingers and the smell reached her nose, suffusing her, nauseating her. "Just lie still. I'll call for help."

Splashes of red clung to Jill's yellow blouse. Beck noticed the torn sleeve and two missing buttons, then thought how strange it was to notice such trivial details at a time like this.

Jill tried to grasp Beck's hand, but her own limp hand couldn't manage the strenuous task. "Josh... Josh..."

Josh! Where was the child? Had Royce Paxton harmed him, too? "Just lie still," Beck said. "I've got to call for help. I'll find Josh."

Mechanically Rebecca Jane Kendrick stood up, walked to the telephone and dialed 911. In a calm, controlled voice she told the basic details and gave directions to her apartment. Then, torn between the desire to stay close to Jill's side and the desperate need to find four-year-old Josh, Beck searched her living room.

"Josh?" Jill moaned.

"I'll find him." Beck tried to reassure, but fear gripped her heart.

"Ms. Kendrick?" a masculine voice called out.

Beck looked up to see her neighbor, Don Brown, standing in the foyer. "Mr. Brown, please don't come in here."

"I heard screams. Are you all right?" he asked.

"I'm fine, but Jill has been badly hurt. I've called for an ambulance and the police. Could you wait outside for them?"

"Yes, of course. But are you sure there's nothing I can do?"

"Nothing but send the ambulance attendants in here as soon as they arrive."

She heard her neighbor walk out, and thanked God her screams had gained someone's attention. Beck left the living room and entered the small, windowless dining room. It stood in silent darkness except for the light from the open doorway reflecting off the mirror-paneled back wall.

Taking several steps, she called softly to the child. "Josh. Josh."

Silence. She flipped on the wall switch, and light from the gleaming silver-and-crystal chandelier illuminated the starkly elegant room. She surveyed the area with one sweeping glance. Josh Yerby stood in the corner, his small body pressed against the beige wall. He stood stiffly. Only the slight movement of his little chest as he breathed in and out testified he was alive. His big blue eyes stared blankly.

Beck moved slowly toward the child. Not wanting to frighten him further, she stopped a few feet away and knelt down to face him. "Josh."

He didn't move or reply.

"Josh, it's all right, honey. I've called for help." She wanted to tell him his mother would be fine, that there was nothing to worry about, nothing to be afraid of anymore. But she couldn't—wouldn't—lie to him. She longed to reach out and take him in her arms, but knew not to.

His body remained perfectly still, but his eyes moved upward toward the sound of Beck's voice as she talked to him.

"Josh, don't be afraid. He's gone. Help is on the way. I'm here and I won't let anyone hurt you."

Soundlessly Josh tumbled forward and grabbed Beck, clutching her around the neck. She seized him and held him fiercely in her arms, whispering soothing words, leaning her head against his where it rested on her shoulder. She stood and carried the child back into the living room.

Beck didn't want Josh to see his mother in such a battered condition, but she needed to reassure Jill that she'd found Josh and he was, at least physically, all right. Holding the trembling child, Beck stood in the doorway.

"Jill, I've found Josh. He's all right."

A low moan came from behind the couch, and Beck's insides knotted. She needed to protect the child from the sight of his mother's brutally beaten body, and yet she longed to comfort the injured woman.

For what seemed like an eternity, Beck stood in the doorway holding Josh, who clung to her with a tenacious grasp. She continued talking to Jill, whose moans and whimpers tormented Beck, making her feel totally helpless.

Finally the police and ambulance arrived. Everything happened quickly then. Jill was placed on a stretcher as the police questioned Beck. When the paramedics moved the stretcher toward the front door, Jill Yerby cried out for Beck.

God, what was she to do? Jill kept calling her name, but Josh refused to release her. Pulling the child out of her arms, she handed him to one of the officers. Josh screamed, thrashing his arms and legs about like an animal gone mad.

"No, baby, don't," Beck said. "I'll be right back."

She could hear the child's screams, a sound more deafening than the sirens. But she went to Jill, trying to stop the paramedics on their flight out the door. Running to keep up with them, she looked down at Jill.

"Beck."

"I'm here."

"Find...Quent Yerby." Jill's grasp on Beck's hand tightened slightly just as they neared the ambulance. "Josh's...uncle."

"Quent Yerby?" Beck released Jill's hand as the paramedics lifted her into the ambulance.

"Promise," Jill whispered.

Beck stood on the sidewalk, the cool March breeze caressing her face, playing with the loose strands of her black hair. "I promise," she said. "I promise I'll find Josh's uncle."

One

So this is The Jungle, Beck thought, stopping just inside the front door. It wasn't quite what she'd expected, and yet it was. She'd half thought the gym would look a bit more like the yuppie athletic clubs she had visited. But, considering the address was in Memphis's Overton Square, she should have been forewarned.

In the center of the enormous room stood a boxing ring where two men danced around, throwing and dodging punches. Several other men, some in sweats, some in shorts, practiced their skills on punching bags. The strong smell of male perspiration mingled with tobacco smoke. Rebecca Jane Kendrick despised both odors.

Bracing herself to invade this masculine domain, she adjusted the perfectly straight collar on her red wool jacket and brushed nonexistent wrinkles out of her black skirt. She'd known confronting Josh's uncle wouldn't be easy, but having to come to *this place* made it more difficult.

She walked slowly, her gaze taking in the barbaric atmosphere of big, manly bodies straining and sweating, their muscles bulging as they made their brutal attacks. She searched for someone, anyone who might be able to tell her if she was in the right place at the right time.

Then she saw him. He stood close to the ring, a ragged cigar hanging from his mouth. While he chewed on the cigar, he seemed to be talking to himself, or to the pair of fighting men who surely couldn't hear him. The short, stocky, partially bald man was the only one in the room not engaged in some sort of strenuous activity.

Beck walked straight over to him and stopped. He didn't seem to notice her. She cleared her throat and moved forward. The man turned around, took the cigar out of his mouth and gaped at her. His brown eyes grew wide as he looked Beck over from head to toe. He let out a low, crude whistle. Beck stiffened. She hated when men did that.

"Yes, ma'am, what can I do for you?" he asked.

Beck felt her face redden and knew the reaction was more out of anger than embarrassment. "I'm looking for someone. I'm told he's usually here this time of day."

"Lucky guy. What's his name?"

"Quent Yerby."

"You looking for Quent?" he asked, shaking his head and grunting. "What's a classy dame like you doing looking for ol' Quent?"

"Mr...."

"Harris. Pete Harris."

"Mr. Harris, my business is with Mr. Yerby. Is he or is he not here?" Beck drew in a deep breath and let it out on an exasperated sigh.

"Whoa. Yes, ma'am, he's here. In the weight room. Back there." Pete nodded in the direction of the open double doors past the row of punching bags. "Should I announce you?" He chuckled, and Beck's stomach knotted tightly.

"Thanks, but that won't be necessary," she said, hoping she sounded more civil than she felt. If she could have found out Quent Yerby's home address, she wouldn't have been forced to come here.

As she walked toward the weight room, she could feel the men watching her. She wanted to scream at them, to call them perverts, but she simply held her head high and strutted right past their leering eyes and drooling mouths. Just as she reached the open double doors, the whistling began, soon followed by several vulgar and totally macho comments. There is nothing on earth more insufferable than Neanderthal men, she thought. Lord, save her from such creatures.

Trying to block the repugnant sounds and odors of The Jungle out of her mind, Beck reminded herself of why she was here. She had promised Jill Yerby that she'd find Josh's uncle, and Beck was a woman who always kept her promises. It had taken Human Services three weeks of inquiries before they'd found out that there was a Quent Yerby in Memphis, and that he was Josh's uncle. Beck wondered why Jill had never mentioned the man until she knew she might be dying.

The bright cleanliness of the weight room surprised Beck. All the equipment appeared shiny and new. A huge, muscle-bound blond lay on a bench, his enormous arms lifting and lowering a weight. When he saw Beck, he smiled. She looked away, her gaze hesitating briefly on the other side of the room where a man with gray hair and a thick mustache tested his fitness on a treadmill.

At the back of the room, a section of the floor was raised, and a row of athletic equipment spanned the wall. Another man rose from a workout bench, his legs straddling the padded surface. He swung his head from side to side, releasing a shower of sweat. He reached out and picked up a white towel from the floor and wiped the moisture from his face, neck and bare chest. Beck couldn't take her eyes off the man. There was something powerful, compelling, even dangerous about him. Could he be Quent Yerby? she wondered, then prayed to a benevolent God that he wasn't. Of course, there was only one way to find out.

She didn't bother approaching either of the other two men. Some instinct that Beck didn't even want to admit existed told her that the big, sweaty, bare-chested man was the one she'd come to see. She made her way across the room, hesitating in front of the steps leading upward. Then it happened. Someone whistled, that damnable wolf whistle. Instinctively she turned around and glared at the blond Adonis who'd ceased his weight lifting and was flexing his muscles while smiling idiotically. She clenched her teeth tightly, trying to resist the urge to tell him to go to hell.

Quent had seen her the minute she walked in, had even sensed her presence before he looked up and saw her. Maybe it was the scent of something sweet and female that had alerted him. A woman in this place was as rare as an air conditioner in Alaska. Oh, sometimes a wife or a girlfriend would find an excuse to drop in, but none of them looked like the tall, elegant brunette who was giving Ted the evil eye. Obviously she'd been offended by his whistle. Her anger was irrational, of course. What had she expected walking into a men's gym looking like some high fashion model straight off the pages of *Vogue?* Correction—The Jungle wasn't a gym anymore, it was now a men's athletic club, or it soon would be when he and Pete finished the remodeling.

When she turned around, threw her shoulders back and tilted her chin, Quent got a good look at her face. He felt like he'd been poleaxed. He stared at her while she moved toward him. With her hair pulled back into a thick bun at the nape of her neck, her slender body clad in a designer suit, and diamonds glittering in her ears, the lady looked badly out of place. She stopped dead still directly in front of him. Long black eyelashes framed her big brown eyes. He'd never seen such beautiful eyes.

Get a hold of yourself, boy, Quent thought. So she's a knockout. You've seen gorgeous women before, you've even had a few. He draped the damp towel around his neck and stood up.

"You looking for somebody in particular, sweet thing?" he asked, a broad smile on his face. Gut instincts told him she'd hate the endearment. Those same instincts told him this woman was bad news and that he needed to put her on the defensive for self-protection. He liked the way she looked—too much for his own good. The stirrings in his body were flooding his mind with X-rated thoughts.

Sweet thing? Sweet thing! Beck felt the blood rush to her head, could hear the roaring in her ears. Clenching her teeth, she took another deep breath. "Are you Quent Yerby?"

"Am I...yeah, I'm Quent Yerby." She was looking for him? This black-haired amazon was looking for him.

Beck closed her eyes momentarily and prayed for patience. She sighed loudly. "I need to speak with you about something extremely important, Mr. Yerby."

"Yeah?" Quent racked his brain trying to figure out what a lady like her would have to talk to him about.

"This is hardly an ideal place to talk." She spoke with her hands in motion and her eyes darting about the room. "I would have contacted you at home, but we weren't able to locate anyone who could give us the address."

He rubbed his chin thoughtfully, puzzled by her comment. "I don't have an apartment at the moment. I'm staying here temporarily."

"I see." Beck tried not to notice how good-looking he was, how blue his eyes were, how broad and thickly muscled his chest was. "Mr. Yerby—"

"Call me Quent, sweet thing."

She winced as if in pain. A dyed-in-the-wool women's libber, he decided, and the thought irritated him. A woman as desirable as this one was made to warm a man's bed, bear his children.... Whoa! Quent didn't like the direction his thoughts were taking.

"Mr. Yerby, I'd appreciate it if we could go somewhere a little more private to talk. Do you, by any chance, have an office?"

"Pete's got an office that we share since I bought half ownership in the gym, but it's a mess right now." He walked over to her and stopped so close that his hand could touch her cheek if he reached out. "Why don't you just tell me what this is all about, Ms.... Ms...."

"Kendrick. Dr. Kendrick."

"Doctor?"

"I'm a child psychologist."

"I'm impressed."

"It would appear that you, Mr. Yerby, are the only living relative of my foster son, Joshua Phillip Yerby."

"I'm *what?*"

"My foster son—"

"Look, lady, I don't know what kind of game you're trying to play here, but I don't have a nephew."

"Your brother, Phillip Yerby, married a young woman, Jill Sawyer, five years ago. He died shortly before the birth of their son, Joshua."

"I had a brother named Phillip, but he wasn't the marrying kind."

"Why is it that you didn't know your brother was married? Why was it that you didn't bother to attend his funeral or try to find out anything about his family?"

"Just who the hell are you?" He couldn't stop looking at her, at those big brown eyes, that long, slender nose, those full, pouty lips. Had someone sent her here as a joke?

"I told you," she snapped, then caught herself sounding shrewish and softened her voice. "I'm Dr. Rebecca Kendrick, and I'm your nephew's foster mother."

"Look, lady—er...Dr. Kendrick—I don't have a nephew. My only living relatives are a couple of cousins who live out in Texas."

"You're mistaken." Beck wished he'd stop looking at her as if he were trying to memorize her face. If he wanted to unnerve her, he was doing a remarkably good job. "I can assure you that your brother married.and fathered a child before his death five years ago."

"Hey, Quent, how about introducing me to your lady friend?" Muscle-bound Ted sauntered over, his boyishly handsome face all smiles as he grinned at Beck.

Quent grabbed Beck's arm and maneuvered her down the steps. "Ted, this is Dr. Kendrick. She's making a house call and she doesn't have time to socialize."

Aggravated by Quent Yerby's macho tactics, Beck halted outside the weight room. "Just what do you think you're doing?"

"I'm showing you to my office," he told her, tugging on her arm and practically dragging her into a small, musty room.

Quent could hear the whistles and comments coming from the gym, and he noticed how ramrod straight Dr. Kendrick stood against the wall inside his cluttered office.

"Would you close the door, please?" she asked.

Quent stuck his head out and yelled, "Why don't you baboons shut up? You're making the lady nervous." He slammed the door so hard it shook. With the door closed, he realized how little light came through the back alley window and quickly turned on the overhead light.

Beck took a quick glance around the office, which looked like a storage area. Variously sized boxes littered the floor, stacks of paper covered the desktop, and a pair of dirty sweats hung over the back of the tattered swivel chair. The one window was small and exceedingly dirty. The large metal garbage can was filled to overflowing.

"Sit down, Doc." Quent pointed to a rusty folding chair near the door.

Beck eyed the chair, wondering what the chances were of it collapsing, perhaps even caving in on itself, when she sat. A stringy cobweb ran from one chair leg to the middle brace. Wishing she could wipe off the seat first, Beck groaned inwardly and sat down.

"The reason I've contacted you, Mr. Yerby, is that I wish to adopt Josh, and I must have your consent to start proceedings." There, she'd said it.

"You and your husband want to adopt this kid you claim is my brother's son?" Quent sat down in the swivel chair and leaned back, clasping his hands together and throwing them behind his neck. Bracing his head in his cupped palms, he rocked back and forth.

Why didn't the man have the decency to put on a shirt? Beck wondered. Didn't he know what he looked like, sitting there in nothing but a pair of nylon trunks? The sight was positively indecent. She couldn't seem to stop staring at him, her eyes focused on the swirl of curly brown hair nestled in the center of his chest. "I—I don't have a husband. I'm—I'm single. *I* want to adopt Josh."

"Why don't you just get married and have some kids of your own?"

She scooted to the edge of the seat, rested her folded hands in her lap and cleared her throat. "I have no intention of ever marrying. I do, however, wish to be a mother. I have a great deal to offer a child. I'm a partner in a very successful clinic, and I have a substantial bank account along with some quite lucrative investments. I have a lovely home—"

"Why this kid?" He stood up, knocking a stack of assorted folders off the side of the desk.

"I care a great deal for Josh. He's been through a very hard time. I can help him." She would not tell this man that she related to his nephew on a level far removed from a professional one. She knew what it meant to be an abused child, could, after all these years, remember the fear, the pain, and finally the salvation of her brother's comforting arms. She wanted to give to Josh what her own brother, Cole, had been able to give her. Peace and stability.

"Want something to drink?"

"What?"

"There's some coffee." He nodded in the direction of the coffeemaker resting on top of a stack of magazines at the edge of the desk. "Or there's cola and milk in the fridge."

Beck looked from the grungy coffeemaker filled with the blackest coffee she'd ever seen to the tiny refrigerator sitting on the floor in the corner. "Nothing for me. Thank you."

"You sure?"

"Yes, I'm quite sure. But please, get yourself something."

Quent knelt down and opened the refrigerator. Beck tried to keep her eyes glued to the ceiling, but they didn't cooperate. She kept stealing glances at his broad shoulders, his narrow waist and his tight buttocks perfectly outlined by the snug-fitting nylon trunks. His legs were long, muscled and hairy. She closed her eyes and shook her head. She didn't know what was wrong with her. She'd never had this reaction to a man. Undoubtedly the atmosphere and circumstances affected her powers of reason.

Quent retrieved a quart carton of two-percent milk from the refrigerator, sat down and took a long swig. Beck watched the thick, lean column of his neck as he drank the milk, fascinated by the way his throat moved when he swallowed. He wiped his mouth with the back of his hand and smiled at her. "So, Doc, what is it you want from me?"

"In order for me to adopt Josh, you'll have to...to give up all rights to him. You'd have to sign—"

"You have the papers with you?"

"What?"

"The papers handing the kid over to you, you got them with you?"

"Well, no, Mr. Yerby, I don't. I had assumed you'd want to meet Josh and make sure that I'm a suitable parent before you just signed him over." Beck stood up, clutched the black leather shoulder bag resting on her hip, and once again straightened nonexistent wrinkles from her skirt.

"I don't know this kid you keep telling me is my nephew. How do I even know he's my brother's son? His mother could have had a dozen men in her life besides Phillip, even if they were married."

Beck crossed one arm over her stomach, absently rubbing the silky fabric of her white blouse between her thumb and forefinger. "I have the marriage license and Josh's birth certificate. And Jill's word."

"Jill?"

"Jill Yerby."

"Where is she anyway? Why'd she give the kid up?"

"Jill's dead."

"Oh."

"I find it strange that you had no idea your brother had a wife and a child on the way when he died."

"Phillip and I hadn't seen each other in over two years when I got word he'd been killed in a motorcycle wreck."

"You didn't even go to his funeral."

"No, I didn't." He had no intention of explaining anything to this woman, this stranger who claimed his brother had left behind a child. Even if it was true and the child was

Phillip's, it didn't mean a thing to him. He didn't want a kid, and especially not Phillip's.

Beck couldn't understand this man's attitude, and didn't even try to rationalize her own feelings of anger and hurt over his indifference. After all, if Quent Yerby wanted Josh, where would that leave her? She should be glad he didn't want the boy, that he seemed perfectly willing to let her follow through with her plans. "It will be necessary for you to meet with Josh's caseworker. She will be able to answer all your questions and provide the necessary paperwork."

"Caseworker?" Quent gulped down the rest of the milk and tossed the carton on top of the garbage heap.

"Elise Zimmerman. She and the agency tracked you down. As a matter of fact, Elise allowed me to approach you today as a personal favor. Under normal circumstances, she would be the one here speaking with you." Beck caressed the dime-size diamond earring in her right ear, nervously twisting it around and around. Elise had bent the rules several times in Josh Yerby's case, and Beck knew she owed her old friend more than she could ever repay. But Elise, Human Services, and even the court would have to admit that Josh would be far better off with her than he ever could be with a man like this.

Quent studied the woman. Obviously he made her nervous. It showed. After her statement about never wanting to marry, he wondered if she disliked *all* men, and not just him in particular.

"I'll tell you what—" The insistent ringing of the telephone interrupted Quent mid-sentence. Rummaging through the clutter atop his desk, he found the phone. "Yeah. Well, hi there, sweet thing. Oh, you know I haven't forgotten about tonight." He looked up and caught Dr. Kendrick glaring at him. He grinned, placed his hand over the phone's mouthpiece, and whispered, "This won't take but a second, Doc. Plans with a friend." He turned around in the chair, his back facing Beck.

Thank God this man isn't interested in taking Josh, she thought. He's totally unsuited to fatherhood. It was apparent that his chief interests in life were his muscles and his lady friends. He'd be a terrible role model for Josh—for any boy. No, the men with whom she'd make sure Josh associated would be cultured, dignified gentlemen. These were the only men Beck had ever allowed in her life. Soft-spoken, gentle, sensitive men were the only kind Beck dated. She'd known before ever setting foot in The Jungle that Quent Yerby was a macho guy whose life was filled with danger and violence. Elise had told her that he'd been a Memphis policeman for fifteen years and had taken a leave of absence a few months ago after fatally shooting a teenage killer.

Quent hung up the phone and smiled at Beck. "Sorry for the interruption, but—"

"No need to apologize," Beck said, looking down at her diamond-studded wristwatch. "I've got to go. I have an appointment across town in an hour. I'll have Elise contact you later today."

She's one cool customer, Quent thought. *She's done her duty by informing me of this kid's existence. She's satisfied her curiosity about what kind of man I am, and is inordinately pleased that she neither likes me nor approves of me. She assumes everything is settled and she'll never have to see me again. But that's where she's wrong.* Leaning forward, he said, "Well, Doc, I've changed my mind. I'd kinda like to meet this kid. I'd like to see for myself if he's Phillip's son."

"What? Why?" She gripped her purse straps, twisting them back and forth.

"Let's just say that if he is my brother's son, I'd like to make sure letting you adopt him would be in his best interest."

Beck's mouth fell open and she simply stared at Quent Yerby. "What possible objections could you have? I assure you my reputation is spotless and my credentials are impeccable."

"Oh, I don't doubt that." A woman, no matter how beautiful, who was as cool as this one, could freeze a man to death at thirty paces. "I'm just wondering if some high-class, man-hating shrink is the right person to raise any boy, let alone a Yerby."

"I'll have you know..." Beck marched over to his desk, her dark eyes bright, her cheeks ruddy, her slender hands balled into fists at her side. "You're insufferable, Mr. Yerby."

"And you're beautiful when you're angry, Dr. Kendrick."

Beck slammed her open palms down on the desk, her statuesque body draped over the disarray of papers, her face only a few inches from his. "Do us both a favor, and don't turn this into a fight. You may think you're some tough stud, but don't let my looks fool you. I'm tough as nails."

"I'm sure you are," he said.

He was grinning, damn him, grinning as if he found the whole thing amusing. She resisted the urge to slap that smug look off his face, feeling panicky that her thoughts had turned violent. She abhorred violence of any kind. God, what was this man doing to her? "If you're so concerned about Josh, then by all means, meet him. Ask him if he wants to stay with me."

"I'm sure he'll say he does. After all he's male, and I can't imagine any guy in his right mind not wanting to stay with you." He leaned his head toward hers, his lips so close that their breaths mingled. Once again his errant thoughts slipped toward the obscene.

Beck's gaze locked with Quent's. She felt hypnotized by his blue eyes, the bluest blue she'd ever seen. She forced herself to break the spell by looking away and concentrating on the rest of his face. His nose was long, broad and wide at the tip. His bottom lip was fuller than the top and creased down the center with a sharp line. The stubble covering his face appeared to be a shade darker than his sandy brown hair. "You say such stupid things, Mr. Yerby."

He wanted to kiss her and had the strangest feeling she wanted to be kissed. "Do your friends call you Rebecca or Becky?"

Realizing she was practically asking to be kissed, Beck stiffened her spine and pushed herself away from his desk and the temptation of his nearness. "My friends don't call me either," she said, turning toward the closed door.

"You're not interested in our becoming friends?" he asked as she took hold of the doorknob.

She hesitated momentarily. "We have nothing in common except Josh. I see no reason why we need to be on friendly terms. It's obvious you don't really like me any more than I like you. You've been baiting me since I spoke to you in the weight room."

He stood up, walked around the desk and caught her by the wrist as she opened the door. "Right on all counts. I don't want the kid, but I think I should meet him. If he is Phillip's—"

"He is."

"I want to meet him, then I'll talk to your Ms. Zimmerman about signing the necessary papers if..."

"If what?"

"If I decide you're the right woman to be the mother of my... nephew."

Two

"So whatcha going to do about the kid?" Pete Harris asked.

"It depends," Quent said, buttoning his pale blue dress shirt.

"Depends on what?"

"On whether or not I think he's my brother's son." Quent draped the navy-and-gold striped tie around his neck.

"Let's say he is Phillip's?"

"Well, all the evidence points in that direction. Burgess said the welfare people did a pretty thorough investigation. Phillip was married to this Jill Sawyer when he got killed, so, legally at least, the kid is my brother's."

"Your old boss down at headquarters have any more information?" Pete popped open a cold can of beer, the frothy contents overflowing onto his hand.

"Oh yeah. Captain Burgess was full of information." Quent knotted his tie and looked in the mirror.

"About the kid?"

"About the kid's mother. It seems Jill Sawyer Yerby was beaten to death three weeks ago in Dr. Rebecca Kendrick's home."

Pete let out a long, low whistle and scratched his chin. "The gorgeous doc didn't tell you anything about that, did she?"

Quent grunted and gave his head a negative shake. "Seems the chief suspect is Jill's ex-boyfriend. According to Dr. Kendrick, Jill told her he was the man who'd attacked her."

"Sounds like a real sweet guy."

"Yeah."

"Could he be the kid's father?"

"Who knows?"

"If he's Phillip's kid, you planning on taking him off the doc's hands?" Pete guzzled the beer quickly, then belched.

"What the hell would I do with a four-year-old?"

"What kind of man will the kid grow up to be with some snobby, straitlaced female bringing him up? He's liable to turn into a little sissy."

"That's not my problem. Phillip had no business getting some girl pregnant and then killing himself on that damned motorcycle. Stupid jerk never did have any sense of responsibility."

"You can't blame the kid for what your brother did to you."

Quent's eyes darkened like the sky before a storm—bright blue turning to gray. He snatched his navy jacket off the metal hanger. "Shut up!"

"Hell's bells, Quent. That was seven years ago. How long you gonna hang on to that hurt?"

Quent rammed his arms into the jacket, jerked on the lapels to straighten the garment, and buttoned the waist-level button. "How many times do I have to tell you? There is no hurt. I just don't want to talk about it."

"What if you like the kid?"

"It won't matter."

"What if he likes you?"

Quent walked toward the door, hesitated momentarily and turned around to face his friend. "I'm going to talk to the doc, see the kid and then tell this Zimmerman woman to do whatever she thinks is best."

Pete followed Quent outside into the small parking lot beside the gym. "I could go with you if you want me to."

Quent opened the door on his red-and-white '65 Chevelle Super Sport. "Thanks, Pete, but I'll be fine."

"I think your gorgeous doc is as tough as you are, old buddy. You might wish you had reinforcements by the time she finishes with you."

Quent slid inside his cherished antique car, rolled down the window, and stuck out his head. "If I actually wanted the kid, she wouldn't have a prayer of winning."

"I appreciate your giving me one more day on this," Beck said as she snapped closed her sleek leather briefcase.

"It's not just me," Elise Zimmerman said. "The whole department is willing to bend over backward to help you with Josh. And no one wants to see you obtain permanent custody of that child more than I do."

"You can't imagine how much I want Josh." Beck felt the emotion clogging her throat.

"You don't think Quent Yerby is going to pose a problem?"

"I don't think so." Beck picked up several files from her desk and neatly arranged them in a stack. "But then, you never can tell with a man like that."

"He didn't impress you as good father material, did he?"

"He didn't impress me as good man material." Beck laughed. Thinking about that macho imbecile Quent Yerby eased the heartache lodged in her throat. "He's a Me-Tarzan-You-Jane type. Did I tell you what he kept calling me?"

" 'Sweet thing,' wasn't it?" Elise smiled, and the warmth of her smile made her pudgy round face almost pretty.

"Then he called some woman on the phone the same thing. Undoubtedly it's his personal endearment for all females." Beck picked up a notepad and pencil.

"Would you have preferred it to be a special endearment for you alone?"

Beck clutched the notepad, then dropped it on the top of her desk. "I can't believe you asked me such a question."

Elise's green eyes sparkled with mischief. "I think you've finally met a real man—"

Beck took the pencil in both hands and broke it in half. "Nonsense!"

"A real man who not only attracts you, but won't let you lead him around by the nose."

"How on earth can a woman as well-educated and re-fined as you are consider men who are well-educated and refined themselves to be boring sissies?"

"I never said such a thing. You're putting words in my mouth. I have absolutely nothing against dignified intellec-tual men. Some of them are wildly sexy and soooo manly."

"But you said—"

"I said that the men you date are the most boring namby-pambies I've ever seen. As close as you are to your brother, I can't understand why you aren't dating guys like him. Af-ter all, Cole Kendrick is one macho hunk."

"I think we've had this discussion before."

"And it always ends the same way, and you always find yourself another nonthreatening bozo who'll gladly jump through hoops for you."

"How did a discussion of Josh's uncle turn into another lecture from you on finding myself a Mr. Right?"

Elise smiled and shook her head. Her bright red curls bounced around her freckled face. Beck thought she looked like a little Irish elf, even though not an ounce of Irish blood flowed in the fourth-generation-German woman's veins.

"Well, when you adopt Josh, you might consider the fact that he'll need a positive male influence in his life."

"I think his Uncle Cole will be the perfect role model, don't you?"

"Mmm-hmm. His Uncle Cole and, perhaps, a new daddy with the same manly qualities."

"Quent Yerby and my brother have absolutely nothing in common."

"The more you talk about Mr. Yerby, the more eager I am to meet him. I've never known you to be so hostile toward anyone. Makes me wonder why."

"Hey, who's the psychologist around here?"

Elise checked her digital watch. "You'd better get a move on if you want to make it home in time to meet Mr. Yerby when he arrives. You did say noon, didn't you?"

"What time is his appointment with you?" Beck asked as she stood up, removed the gray pin-striped jacket from the back of her chair and picked up her silver suede purse.

"Not until four this afternoon." Elise stood and followed Beck out of the office, through the reception area and into the elevator.

"I'm worried how Josh will react to his uncle, especially if Mr. Yerby continues to insist the boy might not be his brother's child."

"He wouldn't be insensitive enough to say that in front of Josh."

"You're right, of course. Not even the rude and crude Quent Yerby could be that cruel."

"What if he likes Josh?"

"I can't imagine anyone not liking Josh. But that shouldn't make any difference. He made it perfectly clear that he's not interested in taking responsibility for a child."

"You did say he questioned your suitability as a parent."

The elevator doors opened. Elise followed Beck outside and onto the parking deck. The late-March wind whirled around them, tousling their hair and teasing their skirts.

"I think he was deliberately trying to provoke me."

"Flirt with you was more like it."

"That, too. He's the type that makes a play for anything female."

"Desperate, huh? This guy must be skinny, with thinning hair, horn-rimmed glasses and elephant ears."

"Lord, no. He's big, muscular and has the bluest . . ."

"Caught ya." Elise smiled, deep dimples darting her cheeks.

Beck unlocked her black Iroc-Z and opened the door. "He's a very attractive man if you like his type."

"Which is?"

"Sort of a cross between Mel Gibson and Clint Eastwood."

Elise grinned. "A guy like that doesn't have to make a play for women. They're probably falling all over him."

"Elise, just remember one thing when you meet Mr. Yerby today."

"What's that?"

"Remember you're my friend."

Elise's laughter echoed off the walls of the quiet parking deck. "You should remember something. Josh might like his Uncle Quent."

Beck inserted the key in the ignition and started the Camaro. She glared at her friend, then slammed the car door.

Quent Yerby stood outside Dr. Rebecca Kendrick's elegant town house. He straightened his tie, unbuttoned and then rebuttoned his jacket. He hadn't been surprised when the address she'd given him turned out to be in Germantown. She was the type who'd live in one of the most exclusive neighborhoods in Memphis. She was a classy lady—everything about her screamed money and good breeding.

He'd passed tennis courts, an Olympic-size pool and a children's playground after he'd driven through the brick portals to this ritzy housing complex. He'd half expected to see a guard at the gates. Obviously Dr. Kendrick would have no trouble giving a child anything money could buy. He, on the other hand, would.

Quent shook his head, trying to erase his errant thoughts. He had no intention of raising a child, not this one or any other. Like his beautiful adversary, he didn't consider marriage a part of his future. Once had been more than enough for him. The memory of his disastrous marriage to Shannon still possessed the power to anger him.

Quent rang the doorbell. The door opened instantly, and he knew she'd been waiting, probably as anxious to get this over with as he was.

"Please come in, Mr. Yerby." She invited him into her home with a sweep of her hand.

He thought the gesture rather old-fashioned. It didn't quite fit her modern feminist image, but the classic charcoal pin-striped suit she wore did. However, the shimmery gray silk blouse softened the severity of the outfit as did the delicate silver bracelet adorning her wrist and the sparkling diamonds in her ears. She'd been wearing the same earrings the other day. He wondered if some man had given them to her. The man who'd turned her off about marriage, perhaps?

Quent followed Beck from the foyer into the living room where she motioned for him to sit down on the brown leather sectional sofa. She sat down in a bamboo-backed wooden chair to his left.

"I thought you'd want to meet Josh first, then we can discuss the situation while Mrs. Avery serves his lunch." Beck crossed her slender ankles, placing one leg behind the other.

"Mrs. Avery?"

"My housekeeper."

Quent gazed around the room, deliberately not looking at Beck. The room possessed the cool, uncluttered refinement of its owner. "Housekeeper, huh?" Figures, he thought, then continued studying his surroundings. Vertical blinds covered the floor-to-ceiling windows, an abstract painting hung over the unused fireplace, and a piece of metal sculpture graced the top of a heavy wooden desk in the corner. A state-of-the-art stereo system graced one wall. He wondered what her taste in music would be. Classical? She probably didn't know the first thing about real music. His kind of music. Jazz.

"Like what you see?" Beck asked.

"Just taking a look," he said. "This place must have cost a fortune to decorate."

"Are you trying to make a point, Mr. Yerby, or are you simply being insulting?"

Damned if he knew! Both, probably. This lady seemed to bring out the worst in him, making him treat her unlike he normally treated other women. He'd always been able to charm the pants off females—literally and figuratively. But with Dr. Rebecca Kendrick, he kept putting his worst foot forward, deliberately baiting her. "Just wondering how a rough-and-tumble little boy would fit in here."

"Josh fits in beautifully. Besides, he's not the rough-and-tumble sort."

"Turning him into a little sissy already?"

Beck crossed her arms and clutched her elbows as she counted to ten. She had no intention of losing her temper with this man, at least not until he'd relinquished any claim he had on Josh. "Josh is a very sensitive child, but hardly a sissy."

"If he's sensitive, I doubt he's my brother's kid."

"Josh has been sorely mistreated during the past two years, and that has caused him to withdraw into himself."

"Why don't you let me judge for myself?" Quent asked, anxious to meet the kid, finish things with the doc and get away from her as fast as he could. She could mean big trouble if he spent much time with her. Ever since she'd invaded The Jungle three days ago, he hadn't been able to keep her out of his thoughts—awake or asleep.

"Certainly." She got up, walked across the room and disappeared down the hallway.

She returned immediately with a small, blond boy clinging to her hand. The child stood rigid, his head down, his shoulder hugging Beck's leg.

"Josh is a bit shy around strangers," she said. And he's very uncomfortable being in this room, Beck thought. She had been giving serious thought to moving, to getting Josh away from the scene of his mother's brutal death.

She knelt so that she faced Josh. Taking his quivering little chin in her hand, she tilted his head up. "Josh, this is Quent Yerby. He's the man I told you about."

Quent stood and looked at the boy. When the child made no reply, either by word or movement, Quent took several tentative steps toward Josh. "Hi." He guessed he should say more, but he wasn't sure what. He didn't know much about kids, hadn't really spent any time around them, but he knew most four-year-olds weren't as quiet and shy as this one.

"Mr. Yerby is your uncle, and he very much wants to meet you," Beck said. "Could you say hello?"

With what appeared to be a tremendous amount of effort, the boy raised his eyes and looked at Quent. Two pairs of vibrant blue eyes met. "Hello," Josh said, his voice a tiny whisper.

Although Quent's facial expression didn't change, his body tightened and the bottom fell out of his stomach. He moved closer to the woman and child, and squatted in order to place himself at the child's level. "Hello, Josh. I'm your Uncle Quent." Quent held out his hand.

When Josh didn't respond, Quent dropped his hand and looked at Beck. She smiled and placed her arm around the child's shoulder. "We're working on our manners." She stood and, still holding Josh's hand, led him to the sofa. Quent followed, and all three sat down, Josh between the two adults.

Quent inspected every inch of the little boy, trying not to be conspicuous in his interest. There was no doubt in his mind that the child was Phillip's. The family resemblance was striking. People had always said how remarkable it was that Quent and Phillip looked so much alike considering they were only half brothers. But then, they had both inherited their blue eyes, their tall muscular bodies and irresistible charm from their father. It was a known fact that Yerby blood was dominant, diluting any inherited traits from the mother.

"Dr. Kendrick tells me you're four years old," Quent said, wondering what a guy talked about to a kid.

Josh shook his head affirmatively, keeping his eyes wide open and riveted to Quent.

"You remind me an awful lot of your father," Quent said. "Of course you don't remember him, do you?"

"No," Josh said.

"Josh is going back to play-school next week," Beck said, hugging the child close to her.

"You like play-school?" Quent asked.

Josh looked at Beck, tears in his eyes. She picked him up and set him in her lap. He clung to her, his little arms draped around her neck.

"I'm sorry. Did I say something wrong?" Quent asked, puzzled by the boy's reaction to his question.

Stroking Josh's back and placing reassuring kisses on the side of his face, Beck forced a smile. "No. It's just that Josh stayed home with me until this week, and he's stayed with Mrs. Avery in the mornings the past few days so I could be in the office a half day. He hasn't been quite ready to return to play-school."

"I see." So, the cool-as-a-cucumber Dr. Kendrick had taken time off from her prestigious job to stay home with the kid after his mother's death. Obviously Josh was as strongly attached to his foster mother as she was to him.

"We're going to give it a try on Monday, aren't we?" With the child still clinging to her, Beck stood and turned to Quent. "Mrs. Avery will fix Josh his lunch while we talk."

Quent leaned back on the sofa and rested his head against the plush leather while Beck excused herself to take Josh into the kitchen. Quent relaxed into the surrounding comfort, crossing his legs at the ankles, putting his hands in his pants pockets and whistling under his breath.

He didn't like this situation one little bit. His only intention in coming here today had been to put an end to things, but he already knew that would be impossible. Josh was his brother's son. That made him Quent's own flesh and blood. He hadn't thought it would matter, but it did. He'd thought the bitterness that had existed between Phillip and him would protect him from feeling anything for the child. It didn't.

And then there was Doc. Dammit all, he wanted her. He wanted to chip away that icy veneer and see what lay beneath. She was hiding something behind that meticulous exterior, something she couldn't conceal when she held Josh in her arms or when she looked at Quent with that hint of vulnerability in her soft brown eyes.

"He's eating his chocolate pudding first," Beck said when she returned carrying a large silver tray.

Quent sat up straight and took his hands out of his pockets. "He's okay then?"

"As okay as a little boy can be, less than a month after witnessing his mother's murder." Beck placed the tray on the large glass coffee table and sat down on the sofa beside Quent. "I'm having tea, but I brought you coffee. I didn't think you'd like hot tea."

"No, I don't. Thanks for the coffee."

Beck handed him a white china cup. "It's black, but I have cream and sugar."

"I take it black."

"That's what I thought."

Quent knew she'd meant her last comment as some sort of slur, but refused to accept her challenge to argue. "I know the basic details about Jill Yerby's death, and about her boyfriend, Royce Paxton."

"You've certainly been busy obtaining information the past few days, haven't you?"

"I'm sure you know my background." Quent moved to the edge of the couch and set his cup on the table. "I know who to go to for the right answers."

"Did your source tell you about the kind of life your sister-in-law and nephew lived before they came back to Memphis?"

"Why don't you tell me? I can see you're dying to lay blame for their misfortune squarely at my feet."

"I do think you must accept partial blame for their situation. After all, if you'd taken the slightest bit of interest in Jill or Josh, they never would have ended up at the mercy of a monster like Royce Paxton."

"I wonder what kind of woman Jill Sawyer Yerby was to have taken up with the likes of a man like Paxton." Quent placed his arms on his legs, his clasped hands resting between his knees.

"She was a desperate young woman with a baby. She had no family, no job and no money." Beck picked up her teacup and sipped the delicate herbal concoction.

"I had no idea my brother had married or that he'd left behind a child. If I'd known—"

"Why didn't you know?"

"Phillip and I had a falling out a couple of years before his accident. The folks were dead, and there wasn't anyone to keep us informed about each other." Quent didn't want to think about his brother or his untimely death at the age of twenty-two. Quent had felt pangs of guilt and remorse when he'd received word that Phillip had died in a motorcycle wreck. He hadn't wanted to know anything else—had deliberately shielded himself from the details of his only brother's life and death.

"A falling out so serious you wouldn't even attend his funeral?" Beck set her cup on the silver tray, turned to Quent Yerby and placed her hand on his arm. "What kind of man are you?"

Quent glared at her hand where it rested on his arm, her long slim fingers curled just above his elbow. God, why had she touched him? He didn't want her sitting so close he could smell the haunting fragrance of her perfume. For the past three days, that damned sweet scent had floated around in his imagination. And now she was touching him.

"I don't think my history with my brother is important. What you need to be concerned about is that a man insane enough to beat his girlfriend to death is on the loose and knows you and Josh can both identify him."

Her hand on his arm tightened. "Do you think I'm not well aware of that fact?" She released his arm, letting her hand fall limply to her side.

"Captain Burgess told me that he's ordered extra surveillance of your town house and the kid's play-school. I know he'd have liked to post a man to guard you both, but he can't."

"He explained all this to me."

"If it's any comfort to you, we're pretty sure Paxton left Memphis in a big hurry. There's always a chance that he'll stay on the run and not come back."

"I realize that Royce Paxton poses a threat, but in the weeks since Jill's death my main concern has been Josh's future."

"Josh's future is the reason I'm here," Quent said, and saw the stricken look on her face. "Tell me about my nephew, and then tell me what your plans are for him."

Beck didn't like the way he'd said that. She had hoped this visit would be simple, but it was apparent that nothing concerning Quent Yerby could ever be simple. Everything about the man irritated her unbearably, and it seemed he thoroughly enjoyed her discomfort. What disturbed her the most was that he reminded her of her brother, and Cole Kendrick was the one man on earth she adored. Oh, Quent didn't look like Cole, but he possessed the same macho charisma, the same air of male confidence and the same deadly sex appeal.

"Well?" Quent asked.

"Josh witnessed Royce Paxton's repeated brutality to Jill during the two years they lived with him. During the last few months, Paxton began abusing Josh. That's when Jill finally worked up enough courage to leave and bring Josh here to Memphis to the shelter, and that's where we met. I do volunteer work there."

"You play psychologist twenty-four hours a day, seven days a week?"

"I don't ever *play* psychologist, Mr. Yerby. I *am* a psychologist, and I'm devoted to my profession."

"Why'd you bring Josh and his mother here to live with you?"

"I wanted to help Jill. She was a pretty, intelligent young woman who'd had some bad breaks."

"Did she know you wanted her kid?"

Beck gasped, her cheeks flushing as she jerked around to face him. Her knee accidentally bumped his. She pulled back and glared at him. "I helped Jill get a part-time job and enroll in night school. The only thing I wanted was to help her and Josh."

"Why does a woman like you want a knocked-around, mixed-up kid like Josh? You want to use him as your own personal guinea pig or something?"

Beck's hand was in midair before she realized her intention and stopped herself. She jumped off the sofa and turned her back to Quent. Crossing her arms over her chest, she grabbed herself in a hug as she paced the floor. She'd almost slapped him! Dammit, why did he have this effect on her? She wasn't a violent woman—she abhorred violence—and yet every time she got near Quent Yerby she wanted to do him physical harm.

She didn't hear him get up and walk across the room, but she felt him standing behind her. She tensed, every nerve in her body alert to his nearness. He grasped her shoulders gently and pulled her back against his chest. She didn't want him to touch her. She didn't think she could bear it.

"I'm sorry," he whispered as he bent his head so that his lips were against her ear. "It was a cruel thing to say, and I know it isn't true."

She wanted to pull away from him, but she didn't. For some strange reason she found comfort in his embrace. The trauma of Jill's brutal death had changed forever Beck's safe, comfortable life. Both she and the child she longed to call her own could still be in danger from the murderer. That fear seldom left Beck's thoughts.

Quent put his arms around her and held her, nestling the back length of her body against his chest. Her head tilted slightly and rested on his shoulder. "I love Josh. I...I have so much to give him," she said.

Oh, Doc, I don't doubt that for a minute. You've got a lot to give, all right, Quent thought. You've got so much in you to give a man and a child. "Josh is going to need a father. If you don't ever intend to marry, who's going to fill that position?"

"I have a brother." Beck knew she shouldn't be standing here with Quent Yerby's arm wrapped around her. More importantly, she shouldn't be enjoying the feel of his hard body pressed against hers.

"How often would Josh be around your brother? Does he live here in Memphis?"

Beck struggled with her own warring senses. The emotional part of her wanted to stay in Quent's comforting embrace, and the sensible part of her knew she had to break free before things got out of hand. When she pulled forward, Quent held her more tightly, then suddenly dropped his arms and released her. Beck turned to face him. "Josh would see my brother about once a month. Cole lives in Florence, Alabama with his wife and children."

"No matter how things turn out about your adopting Josh, I'd like to be a part of his life. Would you agree to that?"

"You've changed your mind since seeing him, haven't you?" Beck realized she felt a tremendous sense of happiness when she should feel concerned that Quent didn't seem willing to just hand Josh over to her and walk away. The fact that meeting his nephew had altered his don't-give-a-damn attitude gave Beck some insight into the real Quent Yerby.

"Crazy, huh? I'm not saying I want to take the kid or anything, it's just..."

"I understand."

"And I'm not saying I think your raising the kid alone would be ideal, either."

At his comment, Beck felt her former animosity toward Quent returning. "Why do you think I'm unsuitable to raise Josh?"

Hell, he didn't want to argue with her. He wanted to pull her back in his arms, throw her on the couch and kiss her senseless. Then he wanted to... "Well, for one thing, look at this town house. It's not very homey, and it sure isn't kid-proof."

Beck looked around at her neat, impeccably decorated living room and saw absolutely nothing wrong with it. "Kid-proof?" she asked. "Josh isn't a loud, rowdy child prone to destruction."

"Probably not after all he's been through, but give him time and he'll turn into a normal boy. That's when this pale carpet turns dark with mud stains and your fancy sculptures get knocked onto the floor when he's throwing a football across the room."

Beck's eyes widened in surprise. "Children should never be allowed to play ball inside."

"Kids do a lot of things they aren't *allowed* to do."

"How do you know so much about children, about little boys?"

"I was a kid once—a rough and rowdy boy to be exact."

"Josh isn't—"

"I know he isn't rough and rowdy right now, and I'm afraid if you raise him he never will be."

"Just what do you mean by that?"

"Well, with a woman like you raising him, he's liable to turn out to be some brainy little sissy."

Beck turned her eyes heavenward, drew in a deep breath, and willed herself not to lose her temper. "And what would he become if you were to raise him?"

"One hundred percent boy."

"More than likely a one hundred percent insensitive macho-idiot redneck." Beck's voice grew louder with each word.

"Is that what you think I am?"

"If the shoe fits..."

"If the—" Quent shook his head, wondering how he'd ever gotten himself into this conversation. Dr. Rebecca Kendrick was the first woman in his life he hadn't been able to charm—the first woman he hadn't even tried to charm. She brought out the absolute worst in him, and he couldn't understand why. Every time he spent more than two minutes alone with her, he was divided between the desire to make love to her and the equally strong desire to run as far and as fast as he could.

"I think I'll be more suitable as a parent than you, Mr. Yerby." Beck's hands moved as she spoke, giving expression to her speech.

"I'm not ready to hand Josh over to you. I'm not in a position to take him right now, but don't go making any permanent plans about his future." Quent turned around and walked out into the foyer.

Beck followed, her high heels clicking on the wooden foyer floor. "I won't give Josh up without a fight. He loves me and feels safe with me. He doesn't even know you."

"He will," Quent said as he opened the front door.

When he walked outside, Beck ran out behind him. "What do you plan to tell Elise?"

"I plan to tell Ms. Zimmerman that I have no objections to your remaining Josh's foster mother, temporarily, while the two of us get better acquainted."

Beck stood on the sidewalk and watched Quent go to his car, unlock it and get in. Before he closed the door, she called out, "Why are you doing this?"

"Damned if I know," he said, slammed the car door and started the engine. Suddenly he cut off the engine, opened the door and got out. He didn't make a move to come toward her.

They stared at each other. Beck's heart pounded as loud and fast as if she'd been running. He kept looking at her, his blue eyes saying things she didn't want to hear. *Turn around and go inside,* she told herself, but she didn't.

"If you need me, you know my number at The Jungle. If I'm not there, leave a message with Pete." Quent got back in the car.

"Why should I need you?" She moved toward his car. She wanted to scream that she didn't need him and never would.

"Royce Paxton is still on the loose, or have you forgotten?"

"I'll call the police if we need protection."

"Fine, but you'll call me, too."

Before she could reply, he slammed the car door. Beck watched him drive away. With mixed feelings of anger and regret and loss, she turned and walked inside her apartment. She closed the door on the outside world, on the insanity and the fear, and on the man who had turned her well-planned life upside down. She couldn't help but wonder what the future held for Josh and her... and Quent Yerby.

Three

Josh held the metal chains tightly as he swung back and forth. Beck stood behind him, giving him an occasional push to keep the swing moving at a moderate speed, allowing him to go only as high as she deemed safe for a child his age. Of all the playground equipment here, he seemed to prefer the swings. During the past two hours, Josh had climbed the monkey bars, shared the seesaw with a neighbor's child, repeatedly downed the slides and crawled over, under, around and through every object made for those specific purposes. The only thing he'd shied away from had been crowded with four other children—the hand-pushed merry-go-round.

Although Josh had made remarkable progress in the month since his mother's death, Beck knew he had a long way to go to full recovery. His return to nursery school had gone off without incident, but his teacher told Beck that he was moody and indifferent. Time and love would help, as would the therapy Josh was receiving from Beck's colleague, Dr. Wayne Moore. But, if Josh were taken away from her, if Quent Yerby didn't allow her to retain custody... Beck couldn't bear to think what might happen to the child she loved more and more each day.

"Higher, Beck," Josh said. "Push me higher."

Beck gave the swing a hefty push and watched as Josh flew into the air. She caught her breath when she saw how high the swing had gone. Her first instinct was to grab it and slow it down, her motherly caution almost overruling her common sense. But the moment she heard Josh's squealing laughter, she relaxed and remembered the moments she'd spent as a child flying higher and higher, up, up, up into the sky.

She wanted Josh's childhood to be filled with laughter, his life to be secure and stable. She didn't want him to ever have to be afraid again. She knew the agonies of having been an abused child, of living in fear of a huge, brutal adult. No bruises or scars disfigured her body, but painful memories were irrevocably etched onto her mind. After all these years, the only man she completely trusted was her older brother Cole.

It wasn't that she disliked men, it was simply that she preferred sweet, gentle teddy bear types—men who didn't raise their voices in anger, men who never used violence to settle problems, intellectual men whose physical presences didn't intimidate her or remind her of her father.

She didn't like Quent Yerby. He was the opposite of all she wanted in a man. And to make matters worse, he was the one person in the world who could take Josh away from her, and the first man in years who had her lying awake at night thinking wanton thoughts.

Dark clouds passed over the sun, obscuring the brightness and warmth of the early April morning. A sudden breeze rippled across the playground kicking up a minuscule storm of leaves and dust. Even though she'd dressed both herself and Josh in pants and sweaters, the unexpected weather change sent a chill through Beck.

As the swing slowed, she grabbed the chains, stopping the motion and obtaining a protest from Josh. "I don't want to stop. Swing me some more."

"Why don't we go back to the house and fix some hot chocolate?" Beck suggested, helping him down to the ground.

Josh pulled away and looked up at her with a resentful glare. "No! I don't want to go."

"It's getting cooler. Look how dark the sky is. I think it might start raining any minute now."

"Then read me a story." Josh pointed at the book sticking out of the top of her unzipped shoulder bag.

Earlier she'd read the Mother Goose rhymes to Josh and some of the neighborhood children while one of the other mothers had supplied homemade cookies to her son's nine playmates.

"I'll read to you when we get home." Beck reached out and took Josh by the hand.

"Read me one right now," he said, jerking his hand free.

Beck laughed, realizing how typically four-year-old Josh was acting. "We'll sit on the bench, I'll read one rhyme, and then we'll go home."

Josh eyed her suspiciously as if there were a trick to her suggestion. He hesitated momentarily, then smiled. "Okay."

Beck sat down on the wood-and-metal bench, pulled the book from her purse and lifted Josh onto her lap. He shifted around making a comfortable nest for himself on top of her legs. She opened the book and read "Ole King Cole."

"Just one more. Please." Josh curled up against her and placed his head on her breast.

Unable to resist his plea, Beck continued to read. Soon several other children gathered around listening to the rhymes. Before she knew it, twenty minutes had passed and Beck finished the last page of her book. The crowd of youngsters applauded and Josh stirred from his half-asleep state.

A loud clap of thunder proclaimed the error of the weatherman's sunny forecast. Mothers began gathering up belongings and herding youngsters toward home. Beck set Josh down on his feet just as a brilliant flash of lightning streaked across the sky, followed by a loud boom of thunder.

"Beck!" he screamed, clutching her leg.

She bent over, placing her arms around him, reassuring him with her touch. "Hey, there's nothing to be afraid of. It's just the clouds bumping heads."

"Oh." He loosened his hold on her leg, but didn't release her.

Beck thought how totally irrational her explanation had been. She knew the scientific reasons for thunder and lightning, and realized, as a parent, she should impart her knowledge to her child. However, the explanation her brother had once given her when she'd been about four seemed far more suitable.

By the time Beck persuaded Josh to take her hand and walk toward the town house, the playground was empty except for one lone man standing near a tree close to the monkey bars. There was something familiar about his tall, lean body and his long, shaggy hair. Beck's heart beat faster. The palms of her hands coated with sweat. He looked like the man she had encountered in her town house last month—the man who had beaten Jill Yerby to death.

Not wanting to frighten Josh or alert him to the man's presence, she began calmly walking away from the playground, and sensed immediately that he was following them. She wanted to grab Josh up in her arms and run. She wanted to scream hysterically for someone to help them. She did neither.

The sky swarmed with menacing black clouds. Beck could hear the roar of her own heartbeat over the distant rumbling thunder. She had to get Josh home before the stranger overtook them.

Shimmering lightning danced on the horizon. Beck quickened her steps, then slowed her pace when she realized Josh's little legs couldn't keep up. She knew *he* was still behind them. She could feel his menacing presence. She thought she heard his footsteps. For the first time in her life, she wished she had a gun.

The wind velocity accelerated, the fierce gust mauling Beck with its chilling breath. Her own town house seemed miles away. It wasn't, but could she reach safety in time? If only she and Josh weren't alone...but they were. Everyone else had hurried home.

"Josh," she called out, trying to make her voice heard over the deafening wind. "I'm going to pick you up and make a run for it before... before it starts raining."

She stopped and lifted Josh onto her hip. With a sidelong glance she scanned the area behind them. The stranger had stopped. He stood by a parked car, his hand in his pocket as if he were retrieving his keys. Could she be wrong? Perhaps this stranger wasn't Royce Paxton. Had she overreacted?

Tiny pinpricks of rain hit her face. Beck tightened her hold on Josh and made a mad dash up the street. The wind moaned, the thunder rumbled and quiet footsteps followed. Whoever he was, he was pursuing them, Beck thought. She quickened her pace, running, seeking escape from danger.

Breathless, her heart racing, her body coated with perspiration, Beck fumbled in her pocket for her door key. Clutching it tightly, she raced up the front steps and inserted the key in the lock. She turned the key and twisted the doorknob. It didn't budge. Dear God, what was wrong? She tried again. Nothing. Then she realized she'd put the key in upside down. She jerked it out of the lock and set Josh down on his feet beside her. He clung to her leg as if he sensed something was terribly wrong.

Beck glanced over her shoulder, praying the man wouldn't be there. Her prayers received a negative answer. The stranger hadn't slowed his steady chase. He was less than a block behind them.

The key fell from her shaking fingers onto the doorstep. *No! No!* she screamed silently. A combination of rain and sweat dampened her hands. She picked up the key, inserted it in the lock and turned the knob.

"Beck?" Josh's tiny voice alerted her to his fear.

"It's all right, honey," she said as she opened the door and shoved him in front of her.

Once inside the foyer, Beck slammed the door, locked and bolted it and secured the extra safety latch. She drew in a deep breath, fell back against the door and let out a loud sigh.

"What's the matter, Beck?" Josh asked, tugging on her pant leg.

"Nothing, honey," she lied. "I just didn't want us to get caught in that horrible rainstorm."

"Oh." He looked up at her with those big blue eyes, so full of trust.

She knelt down, and pulled him into her arms, squeezing tightly. He didn't respond, but didn't pull away, either. "How about that hot chocolate? But first, let's get out of our wet shoes."

"Yeah, I want hot chocolate." He followed Beck's example by untying his sneakers and placing them beside hers on the seat of the oak-and-glass hall tree.

In sock feet, Beck and Josh entered the shiny, modern kitchen. Everything was white and bright and clean. Beck didn't like clutter. She was an everything-in-its-place type of woman. Josh crawled up into one of the chrome dinette chairs while Beck prepared their cocoa.

Something told her that Royce Paxton was still outside, that he was waiting—waiting for the chance to... to silence Josh and her forever. She needed help. She'd call the police... and tell them what? That there was a stranger outside her door waiting to kill her and her foster son? What if Paxton wasn't there anymore? What if the stranger wasn't Paxton? What if...

"Mmm, this is good, Beck." Josh smiled up at her. A ring of brown milk circled his little mouth, and melted marshmallow clung to the end of his nose.

Beck tried not to laugh, but she did, and the laughter released some of the pent-up tension within her. She pulled down a paper towel and cleaned Josh's face. "I think Mrs. Avery left some homemade peanut butter cookies in the cookie jar. Why don't you get a couple to eat with your hot chocolate? I've got to make a phone call."

Beck started out of the kitchen, knowing she had to phone for help, but not wanting Josh to realize what she was doing.

"Where you going?" Josh asked.

"To make a phone call."

"Use the phone up there." He pointed to the white wall phone.

"This is a grown-up business call. I need privacy. Do you understand?"

He shook his head in the negative gesture. "Naw, but it's okay."

She smiled and nodded affirmatively. "Thanks."

Beck hurried out into the hallway, stopping only when she'd reached the front door. She peered through the privacy viewer, praying that the stranger would no longer be there. He was. He stood by her car, the rain pelting his body, soaking his jeans and shirt. It was Royce Paxton. She knew it was.

She turned and ran to her bedroom. With an unsteady hand she picked up the white-and-silver telephone. Her trembling fingers punched out the unfamiliar number, her mind never once questioning why she'd memorized it. She tapped her foot on the white carpet while she listened to the ringing.

Answer the phone, dammit. I need help. I need you.

"The Jungle," Pete Harris said.

"I need to speak to Quent Yerby immediately." She clutched the phone, pure panic spreading through her.

"Yeah, who's calling?"

"Rebecca Kendrick. Please tell Quent I need him. And hurry!"

"There's no sign of him," Captain Burgess told Quent. "I doubt Paxton's within a hundred miles of here."

"Dr. Kendrick says she saw him at the playground, that he followed her and the boy home," Quent reminded his former boss.

"She's a woman, and you know as well as I do that women tend to get a bit hysterical. My men have gone over the area, and I tell you there's no sign of any strange man. Don't you think some of her neighbors would have seen him, too?"

"She's not the hysterical type," Quent said. For some odd reason he felt defensive about the lady in question. "She's calm, cool and collected. Take my word for it, if she said she saw Paxton, she saw Paxton."

"She said she thought it was Paxton." Burgess opened the front door of Beck's town house, then stopped and turned.

"I can post a man for twenty-four hours. That's it. My best offer."

"Fair enough." By that time, Quent knew he could have the doc and Josh moved into his place. If they stayed with him, he'd keep them out of danger. She wouldn't like the idea—hell, she'd hate it and fight him every inch of the way. But, one way or the other, he intended to protect both his nephew and the woman who'd called him for help. Every time he thought about that phone call, he felt a sense of inexplicable male pride. She'd been afraid. She'd needed help. And he'd been the first person she'd called.

"Look, Quent, if Paxton ever does show up, Dr. Kendrick and your nephew could be in for some real trouble."

"He's already shown up, and he'll be back. But when he comes back again, I'll be waiting for him."

"You planning on moving in?"

"Something like that."

Captain Burgess walled his eyes heavenward, grunted and walked out. Quent closed the door behind the police captain and headed for the kitchen. Halfway down the hall, he encountered Rebecca Kendrick coming out of his nephew's bedroom.

"Is he okay?" Quent asked, noting the strained look on her face.

"He's asleep. It's past his nap time."

"He didn't notice the policemen outside, did he?"

"No, but he did ask who you were talking to."

"Didn't he want to know why I was here?"

"He thinks you're here to visit him because you're his uncle." Beck walked toward the kitchen. "Would you care for something to drink? I could make some coffee."

"Thanks," he said, following her. "Instant coffee will be fine."

She filled the kettle with tap water and set it on the stove to boil. Her hands trembled as she reached for the jar of instant coffee. "Thank you for coming so quickly, and for getting the police here."

He stood behind her, watching her slender, unsteady hands place a tea bag in one cup and a heaping spoonful of instant coffee in another. "I told you to call me, didn't I?"

"Captain Burgess doesn't believe the man I saw was Royce Paxton, does he?" Her voice quivered slightly.

"He's placed one of his men to guard you and Josh for the next twenty-four hours." Quent saw the look of disbelief on her face, and knew she was too smart not to figure it out.

"He did that as a favor to you, didn't he?"

"Partly."

"There was a man following Josh and me. He stood outside this house by my car. He just stood there in the rain, watching."

The kettle whistled. Beck gasped. She reached for the kettle, her hands shaking, her whole body shivering. Quent came up behind her, his hard chest pressing against her back. He put his arm around her and removed the kettle from the stove. Taking her by the shoulders, he turned her around and assisted her into one of the dinette chairs.

"Sit down, Doc. Let me fix my coffee and your tea." He allowed his hands to remain on her shoulders for another second, squeezed her reassuringly, then picked up the kettle and poured the steaming hot water into the waiting cups. He placed the tea in front of her and sat down in the chair beside her.

"Thank you," she said, but didn't look directly at him.

He took a sip of his hot black coffee. "For what it's worth, I think you saw Paxton."

She let out a long sigh of relief. "You believe me?"

"I don't think you're the type to imagine things. So, if Paxton dropped by today, he'll be back." Quent took another sip of coffee, wishing it would hurry up and cool off so he could down the whole cup.

"You can't imagine what he did to Jill." Beck shivered, remembering the horrible sight of Jill Yerby's battered face and body.

"Oh, I can imagine," Quent told her, his voice deep and dark, rage just below the surface. "You forget, I was a cop for fifteen years. I've seen it all. All the misery, all the sick, demented minds. All the agony and injustice."

Beck watched the expression on his face while he talked. This man had indeed seen it all, and had felt it all, too. The pain in his voice was apparent, but the torment on his face only hinted at the atrocities he'd witnessed. "How can one human being—" Her voice broke on a sob. She choked back the tears. She couldn't, wouldn't allow herself to fall apart. She was far too strong, too in control to succumb to weakness.

He reached across the table and took her hand, his thumb stroking across her knuckles. "Paxton won't hurt you or Josh. I promise. I'm going to take care of you both, make sure you're safe and out of danger."

She looked at their hands where they lay entwined atop the table. His was big and warm, his fingers long and thick, each knuckle covered with a smattering of brown hair. His grip was gentle, yet strong. "I suppose I should have taken self-defense lessons or gotten a permit for a gun. But...but I hate violence. I..."

He squeezed her hand tightly, then released it. "You don't need a gun. I'm always going to be close by...until Paxton is behind bars where he belongs. But it might not hurt for you to take those self-defense lessons."

Beck picked up her teacup, but before it reached her lips the cup tilted in her hand, spilling the hot liquid onto the front of her red turtleneck sweater. "Oh, no!" She dropped the cup. It hit the glass tabletop with a clang and shattered into pieces. She dabbed at the wet stain spreading across her bosom as she felt the moisture seeping through her sweater and bra.

Quent jumped up, retrieved a dry washcloth from the counter and began patting it over Beck's breasts. "Are you hurt?" he asked. "Did the tea burn you?"

She placed her hand over his where it lay atop the dish-cloth on her chest. "I'm fine. Please. Let me have the cloth."

He looked down and realized he was practically massaging her breast through the damp sweater. He looked up and their eyes met, an intense blue gaze locking onto a sable brown stare. "You're not fine, dammit. You're shaking all over. You've just spilled hot tea all over yourself. You're scared to death. Admit it. What are you the most afraid of—Royce Paxton, or the thought of spending time with me?"

She pulled his hand away from her body and tried to stand up. He didn't move back, so when she stood, their bodies touched from shoulders to knees. "I don't know why I called you."

"Don't you?" She was so tall, he didn't have to look down much to stare her directly in the eye. He liked that she was long-legged and sleek, like a thoroughbred.

She moved against him, trying to push him aside. He stood firm. "Please," she said, her voice pleading, her eyes filled with fear.

"You're afraid of me, aren't you? Of the way I make you feel."

She looked down, wanting to avoid his eyes, those incredible eyes that spoke a language she didn't want to understand but did. She surveyed him from chest to feet. His blue-and-green plaid flannel shirt hugged his big shoulders and strained across his muscular arms. His tight, faded jeans clung to his lean hips and firm legs. He was devastatingly male, every lean, rough and rowdy inch of him. And he was right, damn him. She was afraid of the way he made her feel. "I don't know what you're talking about," she lied.

He took her chin in his big hand and tilted her face upward. "I make you feel like a woman, and for some reason you don't like that."

"You're wrong." She put her hands on his chest, intending to push him away, but she didn't. She told her hands to move, but they didn't. They lay on top of his wildly beating heart.

"Who made you so afraid of men?" he asked, releasing her chin and moving his hand upward to finger one of the diamond studs in her ears. "The guy who gave you these?"

"What?" she gulped.

"Did the guy who gave you the diamonds put you off men for life?"

His hand moved downward, his fingertips lightly brushing her neck. She wanted to scream at him, but the sensation of warmth spreading through her lulled her agitation, his touch mesmerizing her body into compliance. "The man who gave me the earrings is the dearest, most wonderful man in the world."

Quent felt as if she'd punched him in the stomach. Hellfire, he didn't like the idea of her being infatuated with some guy who could afford to give her diamonds when he couldn't afford to give her rhinestones. "Sounds like you're still hung up on him."

"I love him," Beck said. Damned if she'd explain that the diamonds had been a twenty-first birthday present from her big brother. She didn't owe this overbearing, macho man any explanation.

"But you don't intend to marry him?"

"Of course not. We...we don't have that kind of relationship."

"Just what kind of relationship do you have with this man you love?"

Beck smiled, and then laughed. "He's married."

Quent shook his head in bewilderment. "And you find that fact amusing?"

"No. I find you amusing, Mr. Yerby. You assume because I call you for help that I'm lusting after your body, that I can't wait for you to drag me off to the nearest bed and ravish me." She could feel his heartbeat accelerate. Her fingers curled, clutching his shirt.

"Do you like being ravished, Doc? Does your married lover drag you off to his bed often?" He grabbed her, pulling her closer, enclosing her in his strong arms.

"My married lover?" She threw back her head and laughed. "I don't have a lover."

He tightened his hold on her, trapping her hands between their bodies. "Then who is he?"

"My brother," she admitted.

"You were teasing me," he said. "And you think it's damned funny, don't you? Making me think you were in love with some guy."

"My love life is none of your business." She struggled to free herself from his viselike hold.

"Everything about you is my business." He lowered his head. Their lips almost touched; their breaths mingled. "Some madman is stalking you and my brother's child. You called for me when you needed help. You knew I was the man you wanted to protect you."

"I told you that I don't know why I called you." She wiggled and squirmed, but the more she moved, the hotter and tighter the feelings within her grew.

"You know." His lips touched hers, the briefest, lightest caress.

"I don't like you." She stopped squirming.

"Yes, you do." His fingers tangled through her hair, loosening the red ribbon holding the long black mass in a ponytail.

"I called you because you're Josh's uncle." He was going to kiss her, and she could stop him. All she had to do was tell him no.

"And?"

"And what?"

"And what other reason did you call me?"

"No... no other reason."

"Liar."

"Quent," she whispered against his lips, not sure whether she was begging him to stop or to continue.

"Say it again."

"What?"

"My name. I like the way it sounds when you say it."

"Quent..."

His big hand spread out on the back of her head and nudged her face closer. His fingers tightened in her hair. When she opened her mouth to cry out, he covered it with his own, his tongue plunging inside, igniting her. She groaned, accepting his advances, savoring the taste and feel of him, glorying in the hot, warm, giving response of her traitorous body.

While he held her head with one hand, the other slipped down her back, rubbing, massaging, caressing. He moved his hand lower and lower until he reached her hips. He grabbed her and shoved her up against his arousal as he deepened the kiss, his tongue thrusting in and out in a frenzy of desire.

Beck eased her hands up his chest to his shoulders and then around his neck. No one had ever kissed her like this, with such wild abandon. She felt so hot, so incredibly hot. Any minute now she'd burst into flame. She'd never known such overwhelming passion—such raw, basic need, and the thought frightened her. The way Quent made her feel was wrong, wasn't it? She shouldn't want a man so savage, so brutally male.

Quent had never wanted anything in his life as badly as he wanted Dr. Rebecca Kendrick. He'd known his share of women, felt desire and shared passion, but nothing had ever been quite like this—this primeval need to take a woman, to protect her, to cherish her.

He held her close, rubbing one knee between her legs, nudging them apart. She cried into his mouth when he slipped one of his legs between hers. He kissed her again, hard and fast, then released her swollen lips.

"I'll take good care of you," he whispered against her neck. His tongue moved upward to lavish moist attention on her earlobe. "I'll keep you safe and out of danger."

This couldn't be happening, she told herself. She was losing control—something she'd never done. If she didn't stop him soon, she wouldn't be able to handle the situation.

"Quent, please."

"Please what, sweetheart?"

"Please stop." She jerked out of his loose hold and, breathless and flushed, stepped away from him.

"Rebecca?"

She shook her head back and forth in a negative fashion, her face contorting with fear, her dark eyes glistening with unshed tears. "We can't. I can't. I—I don't want this."

His gut instincts told him she was afraid—afraid of him! And dammit all, he couldn't bear that. "Oh, sweetheart, don't be afraid of me. I'd never hurt you."

"I-I'm not—not afraid." But she was. She'd always been afraid of his sort. Men with big bodies and deep voices and huge, powerful fists that could inflict so much pain.

"Don't run away from me." Why was she so afraid? he wondered. At some time, some man had mistreated her badly. If he ever found out who, he'd get revenge for her. He'd make the bastard wish he'd never been born.

"If... if you're going to help us, Josh and me, then you can't do that ever again." She moved farther away from him, backing up against the kitchen counter.

"Oh, I'm going to help you and Josh all right. I plan on moving the two of you into my place tomorrow."

She shook her head again and crossed her arms over her chest. "No. That's out of the question."

"If Paxton comes back, he'll come straight to this town house. He won't know where my apartment is. It'll be harder for him to find you and Josh."

"He found Jill here, and we thought she was safe." Beck plunged her hands into the pockets of her tan twill slacks and leaned against the counter's edge. "Besides, I've been planning to move ever since... Well, living here is a constant reminder to Josh. I think he'll recover more quickly in a whole new environment."

Quent took several tentative steps toward her, then stopped when he saw the look of sheer panic in her eyes. "I agree. So pack and move in with me tomorrow."

"No!"

"Yes."

"I can't live with you."

"Why not?"

"It wouldn't be proper. I'm Josh's foster mother. I'm single. I can't live with a man."

"I'm not just any man, I'm Josh's uncle."

She didn't want to admit how much she wanted Quent Yerby's protection. She knew he was the kind of man who would go to any lengths to take care of his own. And even if she didn't belong to him, Josh did. And she was part of the package. "Isn't there some other way?" she asked.

He realized she wanted to be persuaded, needed him to take the decision out of her hands. She was a strong woman used to being in charge, but for once she was vulnerable and scared. Scared for herself and the child she loved. "I'll call Elise Zimmerman and explain the situation. She'll understand. I'll be a bodyguard for you and Josh until the police catch Royce Paxton."

"Oh, Quent, I—"

"I promise not to jump your bones. Okay?"

Beck tried to laugh, but the sound she emitted was a mirthless imitation of the real thing. "The only thing we have in common is Josh. I want him, and it's become obvious that you want him, too."

Quent wasn't sure exactly how he felt about his brother's son. But now was not the time to worry about the boy's future. Now was the time to make sure Josh had a future. "When Paxton is behind bars, you and I will decide what's best for Josh. Until then, let's call a truce."

"If we stay with you, temporarily, you have to promise to behave."

"Behave?"

"There'll be no repeat performances of today's behavior."

"I can't promise that." He turned and walked toward the door, then stopped and looked back at her. "There's a policeman outside. Just holler if there's a problem of any kind. And call me if you need me."

He walked out the door and down the hall. Beck stood motionless, unable to believe that he was going to walk away without finishing their discussion. Angered by his departure, Beck rushed down the hall after him, catching up just as he opened the front door. A fresh breeze filled the foyer. The after-rain aroma of damp earth saturated the cool afternoon air, and the remnants of April showers covered the world outside.

"Quent Yerby, don't you dare leave like this."

He cocked his head to one side and gave her a sidelong glance. She looked gorgeous standing there with her long black hair disheveled from his lovemaking, her cheeks rosy and her lips swollen from his passion. "Don't worry, sweet thing. I'm not leaving you for good. I'll be back tomorrow to get you and Josh."

"What?"

"My place is small, but we can make do with only one bedroom, can't we? Josh can bunk in with me and you can take the couch."

"One bedroom? Sleep on the couch? No!"

Quent walked out the door and down the front steps toward his car. He stopped on the sidewalk and turned around. Standing in the doorway, Beck glared at him.

"Oh, yeah—try to be ready by noon tomorrow. I don't like to be kept waiting." That said, Quent got in his car.

Beck slammed the front door with such force the walls shook. Damn, obnoxious, overbearing male chauvinist, redneck... She leaned back against the wall, her knees suddenly feeling weak. What was she going to do? Quent expected Josh and her to move in with him tomorrow, and regardless of the protest she'd made, she felt a great sense of relief. With him they'd be out of the constant danger living alone would pose. She had no doubt that Quent could and would protect her and Josh from Royce Paxton. Now all she had to worry about was who was going to protect her from Quent Yerby.

Four

―――――

"**Y**ou're actually going to move in with this guy?" Cole Kendrick asked.

"Yes." Beck cupped an empty mug in both hands as she stared down at the moist tea stains circling the bottom.

"You hardly know him," Cole said, his dark eyes focused on his sister's face. "Lucky and I want you to bring Josh to Florence and stay with us."

Smiling and shaking her head, Beck set the mug down on the kitchen table. "I appreciate your offer, but you know I can't do that."

"If I don't bring you two back with me, Lucky's liable to skin me alive." Cole reached out and placed his hand over Beck's where it lay on the cool glass tabletop.

"I thought I'd made my feelings perfectly clear when you and Lucky came for Jill's funeral." As much as the thought of returning to Florence with Cole appealed to her, Beck knew it was out of the question. For once in her life, she couldn't turn to her brother for help.

"You're my sister, for God's sake, Beck. Don't you know I've been half out of my mind ever since you called last night to tell me about Royce Paxton showing up here yesterday?"

"I love you and your family too much to put any of you in danger. If we stay with you, Paxton will be as much a threat to my niece and nephew as he is to Josh. I will not put anyone else I love in that kind of danger." Her voice quivered with emotion.

Cole didn't reply. When Beck stood up and moved toward the stove, he followed her.

"Do you want another cup of coffee?" she asked as she placed a fresh tea bag in her mug and picked up the kettle from the stove.

"Don't change the subject." Cole placed his big hand on his sister's shoulder. "I understand that you don't want to put my family in danger, but I'm not sure I understand why you're so willing to move in with a perfect stranger."

Beck poured the hot water into her mug. "Quent Yerby isn't a stranger. He's Josh's uncle. And believe me, he's far from perfect." She laughed, a strained, phony little laugh.

"I want to know more about this guy," Cole said. "All you told me over the phone was that he's an ex-cop who owns a gym, that he had no idea his brother had ever married and fathered a child, and that you don't like him."

"That about sums it up." She turned and found herself face-to-face with her brother.

Cole took Beck by the shoulders and squeezed gently. "I can hire a bodyguard for you and Josh. You can stay here in your own home."

"Thank you." Tears formed behind her eyes and lodged in her throat. "But we can't stay here. Every time Josh goes into the living room, he's reminded of what happened there. I've been thinking about moving ever since Jill's death."

"So move, but not in with this Yerby guy. Hell, Beck, what kind of man is he, not even going to his own brother's funeral?"

"I don't know, but I'm willing to give him the benefit of the doubt. After all, we didn't go to our own father's funeral, did we?"

Cole's facial muscles stiffened, and his dark eyes hardened to ebony. "We had our reasons."

"Maybe Quent had his reasons, too."

"I thought you said you didn't like this guy."

"I don't."

"Then why are you defending him? Why are you so willing to move in with him? Aren't you just a little bit afraid of him? After all, he is a man!"

All color vanished from Beck's face. She stifled a gasp, and took in quick, sharp gulps of air. "Damn you!"

Cole grabbed her in his arms and held her securely, rubbing his big hand up and down her back. "I'm sorry, honey. I shouldn't have said that, but I can't understand why you're so eager to move in with this guy when you've been avoiding men most of your life."

"I do not avoid men," Beck said, pulling away from Cole.

He took both of her hands in his, and smiled. "You don't avoid all males, that's true."

"What did you mean by that remark?"

"The males you've been involved with in the past aren't what I'd call men."

Beck pulled her hands out of his and tried to move past him. When she moved, he moved, blocking her. "I am not involved with Quent Yerby, and I don't intend to be. Besides, how do you know he's a *real man?* You haven't even met him."

"You say you don't like him. That's how I know."

"Well, you'll be crazy about him," Beck practically screamed. "The two of you are so much alike."

Cole allowed her to walk past him and out of the kitchen. She didn't stop until she reached her bedroom. Rushing inside to the privacy she so badly needed, Beck slammed the door. Trembling with pent-up anger and fear and frustration, she sat down on the bed and clutched the white satin bedspread in her fists.

She hated to fight with Cole. And now, of all times, she didn't need to have this same old discussion with him. He'd never liked any of her boyfriends. According to him, they'd all been sissies. And maybe he was right—at least, by his own macho standards. She'd tried to explain that those "real men" reminded her too much of her father, and she had never felt comfortable around them. Cole had told her that her deep-seated distrust of virile men was something she'd have to work through. Well, she'd certainly get the chance living with Quent Yerby. He was big and rough and sexy. And she hadn't been able to sleep last night for remembering the kisses they'd shared. The way he made her feel frightened her... yet intrigued her.

"Becky?" Cole stood in the doorway, his head bent, his eyes focused on the white carpet beneath his feet.

"Go away!"

"Ah, now, honey, don't act like this. I'm sorry I said what I did." He moved slowly into the room. "It's just that I've been the one protecting you for as long as I can remember. I want to be sure I can trust this Yerby guy to keep you out of danger."

Cole sat down on the bed beside Beck and placed his hand in the middle of her back. "Hey, Josh and Mrs. Avery are going to come running out of his room wondering why we're yelling at each other."

"Go see if they've got all of Josh's things packed," Beck said. "I'm all right. I don't usually act this childish."

"I know." Cole patted her affectionately on the head. "Now wasn't the time to resurrect old memories. You've got enough problems without having to face your old ghosts."

"Cole."

"What, honey?"

"Staying with Quent Yerby is the safest thing for Josh and me to do. He'll…he'll take care of us." Beck turned and confronted her brother.

Cole looked down at Beck, ran his fingertips across her cheek, and smiled. "You trust this man, don't you?"

"Yes. Don't ask me why, but I do."

"Hmm. I'm going to have to check this guy out and see if I approve."

"Don't you dare!"

"Dare what?" Cole laughed.

"Oh, you smart aleck," Beck sat up and playfully shoved her brother backward. "Get out of my bedroom right now and leave me alone."

"What the hell's going on?" Quent Yerby's deep, angry voice called from the doorway. "If you value your life, buddy, you'll get off that bed and away from the lady as fast as you can."

Cole got up and stood by the bed. Beck watched him turn his head sideways and knew he was trying not to laugh. To keep herself from bursting into hysterical laughter, she buried her face in her hands.

Quent looked from the big, dark man beside the bed to Beck's trembling body. "She's shaking like a leaf. What the hell did you do to her? So help me, if you've touched her, I'll—"

"You must be Quent Yerby," Cole said. "This isn't what it looks like. I admit, I upset Beck, but we'd just made up when you walked in."

Beck uncovered her face and looked up at Quent just in time to see his lips twist into a deadly, predatory snarl. He's angry, she thought. No, he's more than angry, he's jealous!

"For heaven's sakes, Beck, tell him who I am," Cole said.

Laughing, she looked from Cole to Quent and back to Cole. "What's the matter, aren't you willing to fight over me?"

"Fight?" Cole snapped his head around and gave his sister a warning look.

"Would somebody like to tell me what's going on?" Quent asked. "Just who the hell are you and how did you get past the police guard at the front door?"

"I'm Beck's brother, Cole Kendrick," Cole said, offering his hand to the other man.

"Brother?" Quent took the hand proffered him, and the two men exchanged strong handshakes and searching stares.

"I'm Quent Yerby. Josh's uncle."

"I kinda figured that out." Cole reached down and helped Beck to her feet. "Beck says she and Josh are moving in with you today."

"Yeah. It's the safest thing for them to do. Paxton'll be back, and I'll be ready for him."

Cole shook his head affirmatively. "Well, I drove in from Florence early this morning to check on Beck and Josh. Since I'm here, I'll be glad to help you get them moved into your place."

"Thanks." Quent grinned. "From the looks of all those suitcases and boxes out in the foyer, I'm going to need a moving van."

"Well, isn't this nice?" Beck said, staring at the two big men who'd suddenly become so friendly. Both men looked at her, total bafflement written plainly on their faces. She wondered why she thought that Quent's silly, lopsided grin now had a rather endearing, little-boy quality when she'd originally considered it a macho smirk. "One minute you two are ready to kill each other, and now you're acting like old fraternity brothers."

"I didn't know the guy was your brother," Quent said.

"Now that I've met Quent, I agree that staying with him is the best way to keep you and Josh safe," Cole said.

Beck glared at Cole. He rolled his eyes heavenward and whistled. She wanted to strangle him. Not ten minutes ago, he'd been questioning her good judgment in moving in with Quent. Now he was going to help her make that move. Men!

Beck pushed Josh's blond hair back from his forehead. He looked so tiny lying there in his uncle's big bed. She leaned over and kissed his cheek, pulled the sheet over him, and sighed with relief that the day had ended and he was still safe.

She double-checked the night-light before flipping the wall switch, and stood in the open doorway, wanting to stay with the child she loved so dearly. In the first week after Jill's death, Josh had slept with her. She could remember the silent tears he shed, the soundless sobs that racked his little body. Beck couldn't help but wonder how many nights he'd cried himself to sleep when he and his mother had lived with Royce Paxton and had been subjected to his brutality.

Josh would never know abuse ever again, not as long as she lived. She would keep him safe the way Cole had kept her safe so long ago. There were still times, like now, when she could almost see her father's huge fist slamming into her, could almost hear his drunken ravings, could almost feel the horrible pain radiating through her body.

Beck leaned back against the door frame and closed her eyes, trying to blot out the memories. As Cole pointed out so often, the past was dead and gone. There was no point in reliving a childhood she could never change. She had to concentrate on the present, on caring for Josh, on protecting him from Royce Paxton.

She closed the door, leaving a small crack so she could hear Josh if he called out for her. Turning into the living room, Beck shuddered at the sight that met her eyes. Not until she'd walked into his apartment this afternoon had Beck remembered that Quent had just moved in himself a few weeks ago. Suitcases lined the wall nearest the bedroom, boxes filled every available space, and paper sacks cluttered each corner. There were no curtains on the living room windows, and a sheet covered the windows in the bedroom. Thankfully there was no window in the closet-size bathroom, so she wouldn't have to worry about privacy when she showered later tonight.

Beck walked into the room, adeptly maneuvering through the clutter. She could hear the shower running and Quent's mumbled singing. As soon as they'd finished their pizza-and-cola supper, Quent had walked Cole downstairs to his car while she helped Josh with his shower and got him ready for bed. Just as she'd walked out of the bathroom carrying a clean, towel-wrapped Josh, Quent came in, said goodnight to his nephew and headed for the bathroom. He'd said he guessed he should go ahead and take his turn since the three of them would have to share the one bath. She wasn't sure she could ever get used to this: one bathroom, one bedroom, a living room with uncovered windows, and a makeshift kitchen with nothing but a beat-up old refrigerator and a stove with two burned-out eyes.

Beck hated the feeling of being exposed to the world. Even though they were two stories up, above The Jungle no less, she didn't like the idea of their every move visible to any passerby on the street or sidewalk below.

She moved around the room, rummaging through boxes, checking in sacks, looking for something to protect her from exposure to Overton Square. Her fingers took hold of a record album nestled in a box along with other albums and a stack of tapes. Opening the container fully, she couldn't believe what she saw. Miles Davis. Duke Ellington. David Murray. Herbie Mann. George Shearing. Wynton and Ellis Marsalis. She returned the albums and tapes to the box, shaking her head in bewilderment. She simply couldn't believe that Quent Yerby was a jazz lover, too.

Returning her mind to the original search, Beck spied a huge box of Josh's toys, toys she'd bought for him. Quickly she unpacked the box and placed the toys in the two wooden-and-canvas director's chairs pushed up against the wall. Finding her purse on the gigantic old wooden coffee table, she searched the contents until she found her letter opener. Taking the opener, she ripped the boxes apart in appropriate sizes to fit the two long, narrow windows. Working diligently, she placed the cardboard pieces over the glass and taped them into place with the masking tape she'd used to seal her boxes.

Feeling a bit more secure and totally exhausted from the move, Beck sat down on the black vinyl sofa and rested her head against the back cushion. This place was a nightmare! Why hadn't he told her he'd moved into the second story of his gym? Of course, she was the only one who'd had any objections. Cole had loved the gym, and Josh had been absolutely fascinated, especially with the newly added indoor lap pool.

The sound of traffic from the street and music from the bar down the block bombarded the apartment. *Great atmosphere for a child,* she thought. *It's a wonder Josh can sleep for all the racket, especially the sounds coming from downstairs.* Checking her watch, she realized it was almost ten and knew Pete would be closing up anytime now. At least that noise would cease.

Quent stepped out of the shower and dried his hair briskly with a towel, then rubbed the moisture from his body. Running a hand over his smooth jaw, he looked in the medicine cabinet above the sink for his after-shave. He splashed on a liberal amount, then rubbed his hands together to absorb the moisture.

He wondered what Doc was doing right now. Having second thoughts about living with him in his pigsty, no doubt. When he'd moved up here, he hadn't had any idea that she and the kid would be moving in with him. But it probably wouldn't have mattered. The truth was this place was all he could afford since the rent was free. He'd poured all his money into buying half interest in The Jungle, this building included, and in making the renovations that would turn the gym into an athletic club.

He'd never forget the look on her face when she'd realized they would be living over his business. But he had to give her credit for being a good sport. She hadn't griped about a thing, except the uncovered windows. Cole had helped her cover the bedroom windows with a sheet. He guessed he'd have to figure out some way to cover the living room windows. No telling who'd be looking up from the street, and he didn't like the idea of anybody peeping in on Doc. Especially not tonight, when she'd have on nothing but her nightgown—smooth, silky and sheer, the outline of her body visible through the transparent garment.

Quent reached for his briefs and slipped them on, adjusting them to cover his arousal. Thoughts of Dr. Rebecca Jane Kendrick had his body preparing for a pleasure it was sure to be denied. He picked up his jeans off the floor, stepped into them and jerked them over his hips. After fighting with the zipper for a few minutes, he finally managed to close it despite the bulge inside his pants. Damn, this wasn't going to be easy. He couldn't go around like this all the time just because he was sharing an apartment with a beautiful woman. Correction. With the most beautiful woman in the world.

Quent opened the bathroom door and walked into the living room. She was sitting on the couch, her eyes closed, her breathing so soft he thought she was asleep. Barefoot, he made his way across the room without disturbing her. Something was different, but he couldn't figure it out. Then it hit him. She'd covered the windows with cardboard. Scanning the cluttered room, he noticed the leftover pieces of cardboard and the two chairs filled with toys. Inventive female, wasn't she? After a few more days with her, he'd probably find out just how inventive when she started re-arranging his apartment and his life to suit herself. Could he handle that? He'd have to for her sake and for Josh's. It wasn't as if there was anything going on between the two of them. And if something were to happen, it wasn't as if anything permanent would come out of it. The last thing a classy dame like Doc would want was a roughneck ex-cop like him. And the last thing he needed or wanted in his life was a committed relationship with any woman, least of all *her*.

Forcing himself to stop looking, Quent made his way to the kitchen. Giving the small room a once-over, he wondered if there was something he could afford to do to make it a bit more presentable. This place suited him just fine, but he knew it was hardly fit for a woman and a child, especially a woman like Beck who'd moved from a luxurious town house.

Quent opened the refrigerator, took out a carton of milk and gulped down the refreshing liquid.

"Why don't you ever use a glass?" Beck asked as she walked into the room.

Quent finished drinking, wiped his mouth with his hand and returned the carton to the refrigerator. "When a guy lives alone, he doesn't bother with niceties."

"But you're not living alone now, and I would appreciate it if you'd start using a glass. After all, Josh and I will be sharing the milk with you."

"What's the matter, Doc, afraid of germs?"

"Not only is it unsanitary, it's unmannerly."

"Unmannerly?" He grinned, accentuating the tiny creases around his eyes and deepening the shallow cleft in his chin. "What kind of word is that?"

She knew he was laughing at her again, but refused to argue the point. She was dirty, exhausted and nervous. What she needed was a bath and a good night's sleep. "If you're through in the bathroom, I think I'll take a shower."

When she turned to go, he stepped forward, stopping directly behind her. "Before you do, don't you think there are a few things we need to discuss?"

"Such as?" She didn't turn around. The sight of Quent Yerby in nothing but a pair of faded jeans formed irrational thoughts in her mind. Knowing it was best if she didn't look at him again, Beck stood still.

"Such as where we're going to sleep," he said.

Beck swallowed hard, willing her body not to betray her nervousness. "I assumed one of us would sleep with Josh and one of us would sleep on the couch."

"That couch is an instrument of torture to sleep on."

"Then what do you suggest?"

"I'd like to suggest that we share my sleeping bag." Quent noticed the way her shoulders tensed. Even the hint of anything sexual seemed to unnerve her. "But I know you'd never go for that."

"No, I wouldn't."

"You sleep with Josh tonight, and I'll use the sleeping bag in the living room." He took her shoulders in his big hands and pulled her backward toward his body. Surprisingly she didn't resist him. "I'll see what I can do about cleaning out another room up here for another bedroom. Maybe you could bring over those twin beds you had in his room at your place."

"Yes, of course. I think that's a good idea." She moved forward. He released her. "Now, if that's all you wanted to discuss, I'll—"

"That's not all." He took her by the arm and led her into the living room. "Sit down."

She looked at him then, and wished she hadn't. His broad chest was tanned, heavily muscled and covered with an abundance of curly brown hair. At first she couldn't seem to force her eyes to move from his chest, and when she finally did, they moved in the wrong direction. His jeans were indecently tight, leaving little to the imagination. Embarrassed, Beck glanced up and found herself staring into his blue, blue eyes.

He smiled. "Why do I make you so nervous?"

"You—"

He covered her lips with the tip of his index finger. "Don't lie, Doc."

Beck glared at him. He gave her a little push and she fell backward onto the ragged Spanish-style sofa. Quent sat down beside her and placed his arm across the back of the couch, his hand resting precariously close to her neck.

"What else is so urgent that we have to discuss it tonight?" She had to get away from him, from that tempting chest, those big, strong arms and those sexy eyes.

"We need to lay a few ground rules."

"What?"

"Anytime you and Josh are alone up here, you aren't to open the door for anyone without checking to see who it is."

Beck blew out a huffy breath. "What do you think I am, an idiot?"

"From now on, I'll drive you to work and pick you up. I'll also take Josh to and from play-school. I'll give the school strict instructions that only you, I, and Elise Zimmerman have the authority to take Josh."

God, he was bossy! Beck thought. She'd known he'd act like the male chauvinist he so obviously was. "You talk as if you think I don't have good sense."

Ignoring her comment, Quent continued issuing orders. "You'll be under my constant protection, except for work and play-school. You and Josh will go nowhere without me."

"Nowhere?"

She felt the tentative stroke of his fingertips against the side of her neck. Feathery, light, almost indiscernible. Cool shivers rippled through her body.

"From now to the day Royce Paxton is caught and put behind bars, I'm your bodyguard," he said. "Day and night."

She made a tactical error by turning to confront him. When she did, he grasped her neck in his hand, his big fingers lacing through the strands of her long, black hair. He was so close, so incredibly close. She wanted to pull away, to turn from him and escape the desire she saw in his eyes.

"Don't fight me, Doc. Let me take care of you." His fingers played in her hair, his thumb pushing the silken mass against his hand.

"I plan to cooperate. For... for Josh's sake." Touching her that way, with such slow, sensual caresses on her neck and such tender fondling with her hair, he was driving her crazy. She'd never reacted to a man like this. Not once. Not ever. And most certainly not to a man like Quent Yerby. He was big and strong and could so easily hurt her.

Quent felt her withdrawal and couldn't understand what he'd done wrong. He was taking things slow and easy. He was being as gentle and undemanding as he knew how to be. And yet she was still afraid of him. "Beck," he whispered, tightening his hold in her hair and pushing her head toward his.

She struggled momentarily, a look of wariness in her eyes. "Please don't."

Resting his forehead against hers, he clenched his teeth tightly and drew in a deep, deep breath. "I won't hurt you. I'd never hurt you."

She emitted a tiny, gasping cry, fighting a battle within herself, a struggle between her fear and her desire. "I can't, I..."

He touched her lips with his in a movement so unbearably sweet that she responded by closing her eyes and swaying slightly toward him. "You can't imagine how much I want to kiss you," he said, his lips still against hers, his breath entering her mouth.

"Just a kiss," she said pressing her lips closer to his.

"Just a kiss," he agreed, and covered her mouth with his own.

His lips moved over hers, rubbing, pressing, coaxing. In answer to his unspoken plea for her to share in the pleasure, Beck opened her mouth and accepted his thrusting tongue. The sudden invasion flooded her with a hunger she'd never known, and prompted her body to move closer to his, seeking some unknown pleasure. While they shared kiss after kiss, Beck slipped into his embrace, her hands caught between their bodies. She clutched his chest hair in her fingers. With one hand still holding her head, he slid the other down her back to her hips.

Beck moaned. Quent plunged into her mouth once, twice, three times, and then ran the tip of his tongue over her lips. "Kissing you is dangerous."

"Dangerous?" She ached with longing, her whole body preparing for the ancient performance that would soothe the accelerating agony building within her.

"I promised just a kiss," he said, then dusted her face with quick, abandoned kisses. "But I want more. I want to take off your clothes... very slowly. I want to look at you, to touch you all over."

Beck trembled at the imagery his words created. Realizing she wanted the same thing surprised her. "Oh, Quent."

"I want to hold your breasts in my hands. God, I want to kiss them, lick them, suck them." His hands went to the hem of her pullover. "Let me." He pushed the material up until he'd revealed her satiny black bra.

She wanted him to see her, to touch her. She wanted to see him, to touch him. "We shouldn't."

He released the front catch of her bra, and slowly, oh, so slowly peeled the sheer fabric away from her high, full breasts. His eyes focused on the beauty of her naked flesh. "They're as perfect as I thought they'd be."

"They're small," she whispered, wondering why a macho guy like Quent wasn't disappointed in the size. Didn't all *real men* like bosomy women?

"I say they're perfect. Just as perfect as you are. Perfect for me." He pulled her up against him, rubbing her sensitive breasts over his hairy chest. The sensation pumped adrenaline into his bloodstream, quickened his breathing and sent his heart into overdrive.

She clung to him, luxuriating in the feel of his hard, masculine body, the contact of his chest hair with her nipples. "I'm scared, Quent. What's happening to me?"

"We want each other." Had she never known desire? he wondered. What had she felt with other men? The thought that he was the first man to bring her to a fever pitch sent wild surges of possessive longing through him.

"I—I—" She realized that he was right. She did want him. "You aren't the right man for me. You're not... not what I need in my life."

He felt as if she'd slapped him. He was hot and hard and hungry, and she had been a willing participant, responding with loving abandon. When she moved away from him and tried to fasten her bra, he shoved her hands aside and with unsteady fingers hooked her bra and rearranged her pullover. "You're lying. You want me just as badly as I want you. And you need me."

"I'm sorry this happened. It was as much my fault as yours. I don't usually lose control like that."

"You've been under a lot of strain, Doc. Don't beat yourself up over this. We're two consenting adults."

"I'm not consenting," she said as she stood up. "I don't want this to happen again."

Quent got up and walked toward the door. "Take your bath. I'm going downstairs to help Pete close up."

Something strange and alien within her wanted to run to him, to ask him to hold her and kiss her and take care of her. Quent Yerby affected her as no other man ever had. He made her feel out of control, and that was the last thing on earth she needed right now.

"Quent?"

"Sooner or later, Doc, you and I are going to make love. You aren't going to be able to stop it any more than I am. And when it's over, neither one of us will ever be the same again."

She slammed the door in his face, locked and bolted it from inside, then leaned against it. She had agreed to come here, to move into this hellhole, so that Quent could protect Josh and her from Royce Paxton. Although Quent would keep her safe from physical harm, his very presence put her in danger of losing her heart.

Five

Keela Walker handed Beck a cup of spice tea. "You've got fifteen minutes until your next appointment. Take a break."

Beck smiled and accepted the tea from her secretary, who had become a dear friend in the five years they'd worked together. "I see you've brought two cups," Beck said.

"Thought we'd take a break together, and you can bring me up to date on things."

"On what things?" Beck sat down behind her desk and placed the tea in front of her.

"Things like living with the most gorgeous hunk in Memphis." Keela's lively brown eyes sparkled with curiosity.

"If it's not Elise, it's you. What is it with you two? Are you both determined to match me up with a man totally unsuitable for me?" Beck's mind kept telling her that Josh's uncle was definitely *the wrong man,* but her traitorous body insisted she and Quent would be a perfect match.

Keela sat down in a chair facing Beck's desk and took a sip of tea. "How can a guy like Quent Yerby be unsuitable for any red-blooded woman?"

"In the three weeks Josh and I have been staying with Quent, I've realized that my first impression of him was slightly off center, but that doesn't mean I've completely changed my mind about him." Beck picked up her cup and sipped the sweet liquid while she leaned back in her chair and tried to relax. "The only two things we have in common are our love for Josh and our taste in music."

"You thought he was lousy father material, but you've admitted that he's great with Josh."

"When this mess with Royce Paxton is resolved, I think Quent and I may have a problem over Josh's custody."

"The perfect solution would be for the two of you to get married." Keela crossed her legs at the ankles and took another sip of tea.

"I could never marry a man like Quent."

"Could you have an affair with him?"

"Keela!"

The petite brunette laughed and shook her head, bouncing the black strands of her blunt-cut hair. "Aren't you the least bit tempted? How could you not be, with him wandering around without his shirt, even in his shorts or maybe just wrapped in a towel after his shower."

"Keela, you're drooling."

"How much of that great bod have you seen?"

"I refuse to answer such a question."

"Aren't you the least bit curious about what he'd be like in bed?"

"No!" Beck lied. The truth was, she thought of little else when she and Quent were alone at night after putting Josh to bed. Keela was right. She'd been tempted to give in to the feelings that were slowly driving her insane.

"I don't believe—" A loudly ringing telephone interrupted Keela.

"I'll get it. Finish your tea," Beck said. "Hello, Dr. Kendrick speaking. What? When? Where's Josh?"

Keela jumped up, spilling the remainder of her tea on the floor. "What's wrong?"

Speaking into the telephone, Beck said, "Stay with him. I'll be right over."

"For heaven's sake, Beck, tell me what's wrong," Keela demanded.

"Get me your car keys," Beck said running out of her office and into the reception area.

Keela followed quickly. She opened a desk drawer and pulled out her purse. Rummaging inside, she found her keys and gave them to Beck. "Here."

"Thanks." Beck headed for the outside door.

Keela ran after her, stopping her in the hallway. "Where are you going? You know you aren't supposed to leave the building without Quent."

"Call him. He's at home or at The Jungle. Tell him Royce Paxton showed up at Josh's play-school!"

Pete Harris scratched the bald spot on the back of his head as he strolled around leisurely, eyeing every inch of the freshly painted room.

"I can't get over the changes she's made in this place. Three weeks, and it's beginning to look like a real apartment," Pete said, picking up a rust-colored throw pillow from the couch.

"Yeah, she's a domestic whirlwind, all right," Quent said, stretching his long legs out on the newly painted coffee table. "She's had me painting walls, refinishing furniture, dragging rugs and lamps up the stairs, and cleaning out that storage area for an extra bedroom." Just as he'd expected, Dr. Rebecca Jane Kendrick had turned his life upside down. She had purchased a few pieces of furniture and persuaded him to buy a new stove and refrigerator, which he couldn't afford. Finally, he'd had to call a halt when she insisted on completely redecorating the place at her own expense.

"Sounds like she's digging in." Pete put a cigar in his mouth and pulled a lighter from his pants pocket. "Could be she's planning on something permanent."

Quent laughed and slapped the back of the couch with his open palm. "You're wrong there, buddy. The sooner she sees the last of me, the better she'll like it."

"Am I hearing you right? Has the Home Run King actually struck out with the Ice Queen?" Pete lit his cigar.

"Hey, she's not exactly my type, either," Quent said, but admitted to himself that his friend's comment had hit a nerve. He had struck out with Beck, time and again. If he had an ounce of sense, he'd give up. But he couldn't. He wanted her too badly. "Hell, the only things we seem to have in common are Josh and an appreciation for good jazz."

"Well, at least you've been making headway with the kid. I've been watching you with him when you bring him down to the gym. He's getting under your skin." Pete sat down beside Quent and puffed on his cigar.

Quent cupped his chin in the curve of his thumb and forefinger and rubbed his jaw. "He needs a man in his life. Somebody to show him the ropes. Doc's great with him, but—"

"How's she taking it? I mean, is she upset that you and the kid have hit it off like a house afire?"

"Funny thing is she actually approves. She doesn't think I'm the best sort of male influence, but she admits that I'm good for Josh."

"Good for Josh, huh, but not good for her."

"Will you get off the subject? She's staying here so I can protect her and Josh from Paxton. That's all there is to it."

Who was he trying to kid? Quent asked himself. Pete had known him too long to be fooled by half-truths. Since the day his father had brought him to the gym and introduced him to Pete, Quent had shared a special friendship with his father's childhood friend. And when Quent's own father had died, Pete had become a surrogate dad to both Quent and Phillip.

Pete put his hand on Quent's shoulder. "You're the kind of man who should have a wife and some kids. You have a lot to give, and it's been going to waste ever since you divorced Shannon."

Quent pulled away, and Pete's hand fell to his side. "I gave marriage a try once, and we both know what happened."

"All women aren't like Shannon. Instinct tells me that Beck Kendrick is the true-blue sort."

"Think so, do you?"

"Yeah, you'd never come home and find her in bed with another guy. My money says she's a one-man woman."

"Well, she's made it perfectly clear that I'm not that one man." And dammit all, he wanted to be. He knew it didn't make any sense, but the longer he lived under the same roof with Beck, the better he liked her and the more he respected her. And she seemed to feel the same, except when it came to anything intimate. That's when they couldn't agree. He advanced. She retreated. He invited. She declined. And the tension kept building.

"Aw, the harder they fight it, the deeper the feelings." Pete stood up and headed toward the kitchen. "You got a beer in the fridge?"

"A six-pack of your favorite," Quent said, getting up to follow Pete.

"Since when did you start stocking beer just for me?"

"Since Beck Kendrick moved in and started teaching me manners. She says that since you're my friend and business partner and since you spend so much time up here, it's simple courtesy to keep your favorite beverage." Quent loved the look on Pete's face—a startled expression that widened his heavy-lidded eyes and slightly parted his thin lips. The ever-present cigar drooped down from the left corner of his mouth.

Pete's heavily wrinkled face softened when he smiled. "I don't like the idea that some guy is out to hurt her and Josh. What kind of monster beats up on women and kids?"

"Sick guys like Royce Paxton," Quent said.

Pete retrieved a beer from the refrigerator, popped the lid and took several long swigs. "It's been three weeks. Is it possible that Paxton isn't coming back?"

"He'll be back," Quent said. "As soon as he finds out where Beck and Josh are, he'll make his move. To be honest, I'm surprised he hasn't tried something before now."

"Like what?"

"Like going to Josh's play-school or visiting Doc at work."

"Maybe he's too smart. He's got to know how dangerous it would be for him to show up at either place."

"I wish he wasn't so smart."

The telephone rang, and Quent walked into the living room to answer it. "Hello? What? Look, Keela, slow down and tell me again." Quent listened as Beck's secretary explained the situation. "Hellfire!"

"What is it?" Pete asked, grabbing Quent by the arm.

Quent put the phone down and turned to his friend. "That was Beck's secretary. It seems Josh's play-school called. Some strange guy showed up asking to see Josh. He told them he was Josh's uncle. The school supervisor tried to stall the guy, but while she was making a phone call, he disappeared."

"Paxton?"

"Probably. Keela said Beck borrowed her car and is on her way over there." Quent raked his hand through his hair. "Dammit, I've told her to never leave the office without me. What the hell was she thinking, going off on her own like that?"

"I'd say she was thinking about Josh."

"Keela said Beck was going to pick up Josh and take him back to her office. Dammit, doesn't she know Paxton could be following them?" Quent headed for the door. "Lock up for me, will you Pete?"

"Sure. You headed for Josh's play-school?"

"No. To the medical center. She'll have Josh and be headed to her office before I could get to the play-school. Call Burgess and tell him what's going on."

Quent ran out of the apartment, down the stairs and through the gym's back exit. His heart raced, and blood pumped through his body at an accelerated speed. Beck and Josh were in danger. He had to reach them before Paxton did.

Beck drove Keela's Fiero onto the parking deck. Her hands no longer trembled, and her heartbeat had returned to normal, but she still felt uneasy.

"I wanted to stay and finish my picture," Josh whined. "Why'd I have to leave early?"

Beck parked the car and shut off the ignition before turning to the sullen child nestled in the opposite bucket seat. "I told you that Uncle Quent and I have made some special plans."

"What kinda plans?" Josh stuck out his lower lip in a typical childish pout.

"Let's go up to my office, and we'll get Keela to order us something special for lunch." Beck opened the car door and got out.

"Where's Uncle Quent?" Josh asked, crossing his arms over his chest and cutting his eyes in Beck's direction.

"He should be here by the time lunch arrives." Beck slammed the door and began walking around the back of the red Fiero.

A strange sound echoed through the empty parking deck. Beck jerked her head around and listened. Nothing. Then she heard a voice, no, not a voice—voices. She rushed around to the other side of the car, opened the door and helped Josh out.

Could Royce Paxton be hiding here in the parking deck? she wondered. Was one of the voices she heard his? Don't be silly, she told herself, and felt a tremendous amount of relief when two familiar faces came into view. Two receptionists who worked for other doctors in her building rounded the corner, waved and got in a sporty yellow car.

"You're shaking," Josh said, tugging on Beck's hand. "Why're you shaking?"

She took a deep, steadying breath. "I guess I'm just excited about spending the rest of the day with my two favorite guys."

"I like Uncle Quent, too." Josh held Beck's hand tightly as they started walking through the parking deck toward the elevator. "He's my real daddy's brother."

The gunshot rang out loud and clear. A bullet shattered the rear window of the car closest to Beck and Josh. A tall, lanky man ran out from behind a concrete support and aimed his weapon directly at Josh.

Warmth flooded Beck's body. Pinpricks of fear tore at her flesh. The sound of her own chaotic heartbeat drummed in her ears. She jerked Josh in front of her and pushed him behind the green station wagon now missing a rear window. Crouching on all fours, Beck motioned for Josh to get down.

"Beck?" he whispered so quietly the sound was almost inaudible.

"Shh..." Beck put her index finger to her lips in warning.

Paxton was here in the parking deck. With a loaded gun. He'd shot at them. And Beck knew he had every intention of killing them. What was she going to do? She had to get Josh to safety.

"I know where you are," a deep, dark voice called out. "You can't hide from me."

Beck felt Josh shudder. Squatting on her heels, she pulled the child into her arms and hugged him fiercely. Her throat felt dry, her mouth parched. She ran the tip of her wet tongue over her lips.

"If you want to play cat and mouse, it's fine with me," Royce Paxton said.

Beck could hear him walking, moving closer and closer. She knew she couldn't stay where she was and allow that madman to shoot them. If only they could make a dash for the elevator... but there was nothing to protect them from Paxton on the short journey from behind the station wagon to the elevator. Their would-be killer had a clear view.

She took Josh's face in her hand, squeezing his cheeks. Her dark eyes met his bright blue ones, and she tried desperately to convey a message to the child whose life was in her hands. *Trust me. Follow my lead.* As if understanding her silent plea, Josh nodded his head. Crouched in a squat, Beck led the child around to the front of the station wagon. Just as Royce Paxton stepped through the broken glass at the back of the vehicle, Beck grabbed Josh's hand, and they ran in the opposite direction.

Paxton fired his gun again. This time the bullet sailed over Beck's head and hit the concrete wall. Taking Josh with her, she did a nose dive behind a dark blue Continental. Her lower body hit the rough pavement, tearing her panty hose and eating the flesh off her knees. Her mouth opened on a silent cry of pain.

"Bitch!" Paxton fired in her general direction. Again the bullet pierced the mortar wall.

Dear God! Beck couldn't believe this was happening. How could she have been so stupid? Obviously Royce Paxton had set her up. He didn't know where she and Josh were living, so he'd had to plan a way to get to them at Josh's play-school. Why hadn't she changed schools after Jill's death? Why hadn't she or Quent had sense enough to know? Paxton had followed them, and she'd led him into this damned parking deck.

"I'm going to kill Josh first," Paxton said. "I'll just blow his head off."

Josh went stiff in Beck's arms. No, no, she prayed. Don't do this to him. Oh, God, please listen. Please help.

"You, Dr. Kendrick, I'm not going to shoot. Not until I've made you sorry you ever took Jill in and hid her from me." Paxton's voice echoed off the walls.

Salty bile rose in her throat. She took a deep, silent breath, hoping to stem the tide of nausea threatening to overtake her. The unique odors of exhaust fumes and dust filled her nostrils before she smelled the more primitive aroma of her own fear.

Beck could hear Paxton moving around again, walking in their direction. She pulled on Josh's hand, but he wouldn't move. Grasping him by his tiny, stiff shoulders, she shook him gently. When he didn't respond, she shook him a bit harder, then stopped abruptly. Josh's face had turned deathly pale and a fine sheen of perspiration covered his little face. She took him in her arms and stooped low, with her legs drawn close to her body. Practically crawling along the side of the big, blue Lincoln, Beck was hampered by her protective position and the burden of the child she carried.

If only there were some way she could defend herself, Beck thought. But how could an unarmed woman defend herself and her child against a madman with a gun? Oh, Quent, Quent. Please hurry. We need you.

An unnatural quiet descended on the parking deck, and Beck could hear the sound of her own breathing. Paxton wasn't moving. Beck huddled against the side of the blue vehicle and held Josh, stroking his rigid back and kissing his cool, damp face. She looked down at her watch. Eleven-fifteen. Surely someone else would be leaving or entering the medical building soon.

A speeding car shot into the parking deck. The sound of screeching tires and whining breaks bounced off the mortar walls. A car door slammed. A gun fired. Another gun fired.

"Beck, stay where you are!" Quent Yerby yelled.

Quent. Quent. Oh, thank you, God. Beck clutched Josh. Tears of relief flooded her eyes and fell unchecked down her cheeks. Cradling the child in her arms, she began rocking back and forth.

She could hear movement—walking, running. Then more gunshots. Her trembling hands linked together behind Josh's back. What if Quent had been shot? She couldn't bear to think about it. If only she didn't have to stay here and keep Josh safe, she'd go to Quent. An overwhelming need to be at his side, to fight with and for him, aroused deep emotional needs within Beck she'd never known. Her concern for Quent wasn't simply that of one human being for another. It was an instinctive desire to keep her mate safe from harm.

Sirens shrilled loudly as police cars barreled onto the parking deck. Looking beneath the Lincoln, Beck saw the bottom half of three cars and a dozen feet and legs hustling in every direction. She could hear talking—orders, shouts, curses. Then she heard Quent's voice and knew he was alive.

"Search the entire parking lot. Every level. I can't find the bastard anywhere. Some of you men go inside the medical building."

Beck looked up and saw Quent come around the car and walk toward her. She tried to stand, but her knees gave way. Suddenly she felt herself being lifted to her feet, and the extra weight of Josh's tiny body taken from her. Strong arms circled her waist, and she fell against the hard, warm body that cradled her. Shutting her eyes momentarily, she said a prayer of thanks.

She opened her eyes and saw that Quent had positioned Josh on his hip and the child lay against the big man's chest.

"It's all right," Quent said. "You're both safe." He hugged the child and the woman close to him.

"Paxton?" Beck asked.

"The police are looking for him."

"Oh, Quent." Fresh tears filled her eyes.

"Come on. Let's get you and Josh inside."

Beck forced her unsteady legs to move. Quent walked slowly, his strong arm supporting her. It seemed an eternity before they entered the elevator.

"Hey, pal." Quent nudged Josh, but the child didn't move.

"Paxton said some horrible things," Beck said. "And Josh heard every word."

"You're safe now, big boy." Quent lowered his head to rest against his nephew's soft blond curls. "Uncle Quent's here to take care of you and Beck."

Josh burrowed into Quent's body, his tiny arms clinging to the man's neck. The tears in Beck's eyes streamed down her face as she gulped huge sobs. Josh was safe. Quent was safe, and so was she. At least for the time being.

"It was my fault," Beck said. "I didn't stop and think until it was too late. Oh, Quent, I'm so sorry."

"Don't, baby. Don't." He turned to her. She looked up at him.

"If only I'd followed your instructions." The whole world vanished except for Quent Yerby's startling eyes. She felt herself falling into their clear, honest depths.

"You were frightened. You acted on impulse."

He lowered his head until his lips touched hers. She ran a trembling hand over his jaw. Then he kissed her, tenderly. Unbearably sweet the kiss went on and on. Suddenly the elevator doors opened. The kiss ended, but Quent didn't relinquish his hold on the woman in his arms.

Beck knew they had to face the police and endless questions, and that they would have to have Josh checked to make sure he hadn't gone into secondary shock. She needed to take off her panty hose and clean her raw and bleeding knees. But all she wanted to do was go home—home with the child and the man she loved.

Six

The room was dark except for the glow coming from the night-light beside Josh's bed. With his elbows resting on his knees and his big hands braced against his jawline, Quent Yerby sat on the matching twin bed and watched Beck Kendrick as she held his nephew in her arms. The child had been asleep for quite some time, but Beck refused to let go of him.

Nothing had prepared Quent for what he was feeling at this precise moment. Not all the years on the police force when he'd faced every kind of human being and every element of human nature. Not his wife's betrayal and their bitter divorce. Not even the death of the teenage killer Quent had been forced to shoot less than a year ago.

Nothing had ever been as important, as essential to his existence, as keeping Beck and Josh out of danger. He'd never known he could feel so deeply, so completely, about two people who'd been a part of his life for less than two months. He felt so much for his little nephew—love, pity, concern, and an overwhelming desire to give the child a normal, happy life. His feelings for Beck were just as strong, but not as simple. He wanted her night and day. His desire had become a tangible thing, an ache deep inside, a throbbing physical longing. But it was more than wanting to make love to her—it was a possessive, protective compulsion.

Watching her tonight created mixed feelings within Quent. The fact that she and Josh were safely nestled together in his apartment where he could guard them filled his heart with a warm contentment. However, the pungent, feminine smell of Beck's body and the enticement of her sultry mouth, her disheveled black hair and her soft, round curves tormented him. She was such a sweet temptation.

Earlier that day, they'd all endured a nightmare when Royce Paxton had tricked Beck into putting herself and Josh within his reach. Quent had been half out of his mind with fear. Thank God, he'd reached them in time. But the emotional damage Paxton inflicted would take a long time to heal. Josh's therapist, Dr. Moore, had examined him and reassured Beck and Quent that Josh had not gone into secondary shock, and the best thing they could do was take him home. Beck's colleague had gone on to explain that what Josh needed was continued love and care.

They'd brought him home, gotten him to drink some chocolate milk, bathed him and put him to bed. He'd clung to Beck as if her touch alone could protect him from the memories of Royce Paxton's brutality and vicious threats. Twice Quent had started to leave the bedroom, but Josh had called out his name each time. It became apparent to Quent and Beck that the little boy needed both of them to feel completely secure. And so Quent had stood vigil over the woman and child who'd become his own, and as the hours passed and evening turned to night, Josh finally slept.

Watching her now, Quent realized how exhausted Beck must be. Her eyelids closed, her breathing slowed and her tight hold on Josh loosened slightly. What she needs, Quent thought, is a warm bath, a hot cup of her favorite tea, her scraped knees doctored and a good night's sleep. But he knew she wouldn't do these things for herself. She was too tired and too concerned about Josh to think of herself.

Quent stood up and moved toward the other bed. He looked down at Beck. She needed him, and he had every intention of taking care of her. He lifted her into his arms. Snuggling against his chest, she sighed and slipped her arm around his neck. As he moved away from the bed, she opened her eyes and smiled.

"What are you doing?" she asked, her voice soft with sleep.

I'm taking care of you, he wanted to say, but instead he smiled back at her, kissed her forehead and said, "We need to see about your knees. You don't want them getting infected."

"What about Josh?" She turned her head in order to get a glimpse of the child.

Quent walked through the doorway, leaving the door open behind him. "Josh is fast asleep. If he makes a whimper, I'll hear him." With Beck held securely in his arms, Quent moved into the living room.

"I can go into the bathroom and clean my knees," Beck said as Quent deposited her on the couch.

"You stay right here. I'll take care of... everything."

Half-asleep and bone weary, Beck didn't have the strength to resist his kindness. "Thank you."

Within minutes Quent came out of the bathroom carrying a pan of warm water, a wash cloth, peroxide, medicated cream and soft gauze bandages. Beck thought he looked like a walking medicine cabinet.

NO RISK, NO OBLIGATION TO BUY... NOW OR EVER!

GUARANTEED

PLAY "ROLL A DOUBLE" AND GET AS MANY AS SIX GIFTS!

HERE'S HOW TO PLAY:

1. Peel off label from front cover. Place it in space provided at right. With a coin, carefully scratch off the silver dice. This makes you eligible to receive one or more free books, and possibly other gifts, depending on what is revealed beneath the scratch-off area.

2. You'll receive brand-new Silhouette Desire® novels. When you return this card, we'll rush you the books and gifts you qualify for ABSOLUTELY FREE!

3. Then, if we don't hear from you, every month we'll send you 6 additional novels to read and enjoy. You can return them and owe nothing, but if you decide to keep them, you'll pay only $2.47 per book—a savings of 28¢ each off the cover price.

4. When you subscribe to the Silhouette Reader Service™, you'll also get our newsletter, as well as additional free gifts from time to time.

5. You must be completely satisfied. You may cancel at any time simply by sending us a note or a shipping statement marked "cancel" or by returning any shipment to us at our expense.

You'll look like a million dollars when you wear this elegant necklace! It's a generous 20 inches long and each link is double-soldered for strength and durability.

"ROLL A DOUBLE!"

PLACE LABEL HERE

SCRATCH HERE

SEE CLAIM CHART BELOW

225 CIS ACLR
(U-SIL-D-09/91)

YES! I have placed my label from the front cover into the space provided above and scratched off the silver dice. Please rush me the free book(s) and gift(s) that I am entitled to. I understand that I am under no obligation to purchase any books, as explained on the opposite page.

NAME

ADDRESS   APT,

CITY   STATE   ZIP CODE

SILHOUETTE "NO RISK" GUARANTEE

- You're not required to buy a single book—ever!
- You must be completely satisfied or you may cancel at any time simply by sending us a note or a shipping statement marked "cancel" or by returning any shipment to us at our cost. Either way, you will receive no more books; you'll have no obligation to buy.
- The free book(s) and gift(s) you claimed on this "Roll A Double" offer remain yours to keep no matter what you decide.

If offer card is missing, please write to:
Silhouette Reader Service, 3010 Walden Ave., P.O. Box 1867, Buffalo, N.Y. 14269-1867

DETACH AND MAIL CARD TODAY!

He sat down on the edge of the coffee table and placed the armload of equipment by his side. He touched the tattered silky material covering her legs. "Are these stockings or panty hose?"

"Panty hose." She sighed as his big hands moved with incredible tenderness up her thighs.

"We're going to have to get you out of these," he said, his hands going behind her knees to lift her.

"I . . . I can do that without any help," she said and tried to stand. The room seemed to spin around and around. She grabbed his shoulders to steady herself and quickly sat back down. "Maybe I can't."

He reached out and ran the tip of his finger over her cheek. "It's all right. Let me do it."

Beck nodded in agreement. When she felt Quent's hands lifting her onto her feet again, she stared at him, her dark eyes questioning his actions.

While sitting on the coffee table, he placed her hands on his shoulders. "Brace yourself on me while I get these things off."

His hands moved slowly up and under her skirt. Beck closed her eyes and trembled at the touch of his hard, callused flesh against her outer thighs. Slowly, so very slowly, Quent gripped the waistband of her panty hose and maneuvered them downward.

She sighed loudly.

"Did I hurt you?" He clasped the sides of her thighs.

Embarrassed that she'd succumbed to the pleasure of his touch and had alerted him to her feelings, Beck shook her head no.

"Almost done." Hurriedly he slipped her panty hose down around her ankles. "Lift your foot."

Silently obeying, Beck lifted one foot and then the other, allowing Quent to remove the tattered hose. "Thank you."

He eased her down on the couch, lifted her legs and placed them across his lap. The sight of her torn flesh ignited anew his rage against Royce Paxton. Unaware that his fingers were biting into the soft flesh of her calves just below her knees, Quent jumped when Beck cried out.

"Dammit, Beck, I'm sorry. I didn't mean to hurt you. It's just that I can't stand the thought of what Paxton put you through."

Hot moisture formed in Beck's eyes. She swallowed hard. Clenching her teeth tightly, she willed herself not to cry. His concern touched her deeply, and she wanted more than anything to throw herself into his arms and beg him to hold her forever.

Quent dipped the washcloth in the warm water, wrung out the excess and bathed the dirt and dried blood from her legs. "Tell me if I hurt you."

"You're not hurting me." She didn't want to start crying again, but his gentle compassion was almost her undoing.

Tenderly he cleaned her legs with water and peroxide, then spread a fine layer of antiseptic cream over the raw surface. "I think we should bandage them. Just for tonight."

"Yes, I think so, too." After putting the dressing on her knees, Quent lifted her in his arms again. Before she could say a word, he told her, "You need a sponge bath."

"What?" Beck began wiggling. "No, Quent. Put me down. I can go to the bathroom by myself." The thought that he intended to carry her into the bathroom, strip her and then bathe her awakened all of Beck's self-protective instincts.

Ignoring her command, he walked to the bathroom, kicked open the door and carried her inside. "Stop squirming or I'll drop you."

"What do you think you're doing now?" She swatted at his hands where they'd begun the task of unbuttoning her blouse.

"Helping you get ready for your bath," he said, setting her on her feet.

She jerked away from him. "I can undress myself, thank you very much."

Quent looked at her and laughed. "All right, sweet thing. I'll leave you on your own to clean up. Just be careful of those bandages."

Beck sighed with relief. She didn't know what she would have done if he'd insisted on staying. The very thought sent chills through her body. "Go check on Josh. I'll be fine."

Quent hesitated at the door. "I'll check on Josh, then fix you some tea. If you're not out in fifteen minutes, I'll come back in here after you."

"Go. Go." Beck shooed him away with a backward sweep of her hands.

She closed the door and leaned against it. A sponge bath? No. She longed for a long, hot soak in a bathtub, but since Quent's apartment only had a shower, she'd have to make do. Damn! She'd forgotten all about her bandaged legs. Well, even a shower was out of the question tonight— though maybe not. She could always rebandage her knees.

She turned on the shower, gave the water temperature time to adjust, then carefully removed the dressings from her legs and stepped inside. God, the warm water felt heavenly. Clean. Refreshing. Soothing.

The water stung her battered knees, but she ignored the pain. The overall pleasure diluted the discomfort. She suddenly realized how good it was to be alive and safe. But how long would she be safe? How long could she keep Josh safe? Royce Paxton was a determined man. She knew he wouldn't give up. If only the police could catch him and put him behind bars. But he was shrewd. She was an intelligent, trained professional, and yet he'd been able to trick her into placing herself and Josh in danger. She shivered at the thought of her own stupidity and the possibility that she might let her emotions get in the way of her good judgment again.

But Quent had arrived in time to save them. From now on, she would listen to him. He, too, was a trained professional. As a police officer, he'd handled men like Royce Paxton. He knew how their twisted minds worked.

Well, Rebecca Jane, you're going to have to depend on a man—a big, rugged man, she told herself. For the first time in your life, you're going to have to trust a man other than Cole. She couldn't understand what it was about Quent Yerby that made her feel so secure. She was attracted to him physically, but didn't want to be. When this nightmare ended, she and Quent would have to go on with their separate lives, having Josh as their only connection.

Beck heard the loud pounding on the door.

"Tea's ready," Quent yelled. "You coming out, or am I coming in?"

"Don't you dare come in here!"

"Then you'd better get your fanny out here fast."

She turned off the shower, grabbed for a towel and wrapped it around her wet hair. "I'm drying off now."

"Did you ruin those bandages?"

Beck looked down at her wet knees. "No, I didn't." Hurriedly she dried off and applied clean dressings. Then she realized she didn't have any fresh clothes in the bathroom, not even a housecoat. "Quent!"

"What?"

"I need some clothes."

"My bathrobe's hanging on the back of the door. Just put that on."

"I want my own clothes."

"Just put on the bathrobe. Your tea's getting cold."

"Please, Quent. Get me something of mine to put on."

"No." He knew he was acting like a stubborn jackass, but he wanted to see her in his bathrobe. He'd fantasized about the sight of her wearing nothing but that ragged piece of blue terry cloth. He liked the idea that she'd be totally naked beneath something of his.

Pausing to allow her anger to subside, Beck wondered why Quent was being so hardheaded. She jerked the bathrobe off the hook and slipped her arms through the sleeves. The sleeves covered her hands so she rolled them up to her wrists. Taking a deep breath, she tied the belt and opened the bathroom door.

He had turned off the lamps, and light from the kitchen and from the streetlights outside cast a mellow haze over the room. The exotic strains of flute, piano and horn permeated the room with a jazzy rendition of "Scheherazade." She could smell the delicious spices that flavored her favorite tea.

Quent Yerby stood by the couch. He looked at her, a mixture of anticipation and wariness in his eyes.

"I fixed us both some tea." He pointed down at the refreshments on the coffee table. "And brought you some of those little crackers you like so much."

"Melba toast."

"Yeah."

"Is that my George Shearing tape or is it yours?"

"Yours. I've noticed you play it a lot, so I thought it might help you relax."

"Thanks."

She stood in the doorway, the bathroom light silhouetting her very feminine form cocooned within his bathrobe. The reality was better than the fantasy. She was unbearably beautiful. No makeup, a towel wrapped turban-fashion around her head, white bandages on her knees, and dressed in a man's oversize robe—she looked like a dream. His dream. If only he had the right to go to her, to ease the robe off her body and take her in his arms. If only she'd allow him the privilege of making love to her. And it would be a privilege. She wasn't the kind of woman who'd give herself indiscriminately. Quent knew what a rare treasure she was.

"Come sit down," he said.

She obeyed, moving toward him slowly, and together they sat down side by side. He handed her a cup of tea. She sipped the warm liquid, savoring the spicy taste.

"Thank you. This is wonderful."

"Feeling better?" He picked up his cup.

"Much." She reached out for a piece of Melba toast.

"After you finish your tea, what you need is a good night's rest."

"I doubt if I'll be able to sleep," she said, clutching the teacup. "I'm almost afraid to close my eyes." She nibbled on the dry toast.

Quent put his cup down and took Beck by the shoulders. "I'm not going to let Paxton hurt you or Josh. Believe me."

Easing away from him, Beck placed her cup beside his on the table. He took her hands and tugged her forward. She allowed him to pull her into his arms. She went willingly, happily, the feel of his warm strength reassuring her that she was alive and well and safe.

"I believe you. Today wouldn't have happened if I'd listened to your instructions," she said. "I never should have left the office without you."

He kissed the top of her head where it rested on his chest. "Hush. It's over. You won't make the same mistake again."

She pulled back slightly and looked up at him. The depth of caring she saw in his eyes satisfied a deep-rooted need within her. "I never thought I'd say this, but I'm so glad Josh and I have you."

Quent caught his breath. For a moment he thought his heart had stopped beating. "I'm the one who's glad I have the two of you." He lifted her onto his lap.

"Today, when Paxton was stalking us, when he kept shooting at us..."

"Shh... Try to put it out of your mind." He lavished tiny, loving kisses all over her face.

"I prayed for you to help us." The tears she'd held in check for so many hours began to emerge. First they filled her eyes and wet her lashes, then fell like raindrops.

"Oh, baby, don't." Quent took her face in his big hands. "I can't bear to see you hurting like this."

His mouth descended. Her lips parted. And he kissed her. Tenderly. Hot and unbearably sweet. It was a kiss to soothe the hurt, to arouse the senses, to claim sole possession.

He lifted her in his arms and carried her to her bedroom. She made no protest when he reached down and pulled back the covers, then deposited her on the bed. He stood over her—big, powerful and aroused. Beck lifted her arms and opened them to him.

"Rebecca Jane Kendrick, I want you more than I've ever wanted anything in my life," he said as if making a vow before God.

"Don't leave me," she pleaded. "Please."

"God, woman, do you have any idea what you're asking?"

"I'm asking for comfort. I feel so safe in your arms."

Hellfire! She was asking for comfort and safety when he felt like a corralled stallion who hadn't been allowed near a mare in months.

Quent hesitated momentarily, then sat down on the bed beside her. She dropped her outstretched arms and looked at him with dark, moist eyes. Eyes that mesmerized him.

"I...I need you." She uttered the words on a whisper-soft breath, and lowered her head. Her nervous fingers clutched at the satiny pink sheet.

He needed her, too. Needed to be inside her, loving her, taking her to heights of physical pleasure. But she wasn't asking for sex, she was asking for comfort. "Do you trust me?" he asked.

Without hesitation she replied, "Yes."

"Then trust me to take care of you. Trust me not to hurt you."

He moved over, pulled her into his arms, and rested his chin on the top of her head. Damn, this is crazy, he thought. *How am I going to stop myself from taking her?* This woman, this beautiful, desirable woman he wanted so desperately would never forgive him if he took advantage of her tonight of all nights. She was weak and tired and very vulnerable. The situation called for tenderness, not passion. She needed him, and he intended to take good care of her.

He tilted her chin upward. They gazed into each other's eyes, silently exchanging promises. His lips covered hers with gentle abandon, his tongue tracing the outline of her soft mouth, nudging it open. She sighed when he slipped it inside, and her hands crept up his muscular arms until they reached his broad shoulders. Gripping the back of her head, he deepened the kiss and his body shook with repressed desire.

Summoning a strength he didn't know he possessed, Quent ended the kiss. With his heartbeat racing, his breathing shallow and his forehead coated in perspiration, he rested his cheek against hers.

Beck released her tight hold, allowing her hands to roam up and down his broad back, her fingertips making tiny taps over his spine. "Talk to me," she said.

He was hot and hard and hurting, and she wanted him to talk to her? Damn females. Damn this one in particular. She had stormed into his world—his perfectly contented life—introduced him to a child he hadn't wanted to love, rearranged his whole life, decorated his apartment and placed him in a perpetual state of arousal!

"I'm not good at small talk," he said, his voice slightly rougher than he'd intended. Hell, frustration had a way of making a man less than pleasant.

"No, I mean really talk to me. Tell me about yourself."

What was it with women? he wondered. Why did they want to know a man's most intimate secrets? Of course most of the women he'd known hadn't really cared, they'd just been nosy. "What do you want to know?"

Beck pulled both pillows up against the headboard, scooted backward, and snuggled into a comfortable position. "You usually make love to a woman when she asks you to share her bed, don't you?"

Well, she was direct, he thought, and she was well aware that this type of companionship was alien to him. "Yeah."

"How long have you been divorced?"

"Seven years."

Beck reached out for his hand. When she wrapped her fingers around his, he looked at her with suspicion in his eyes. "Tell me about her."

Was she crazy? He didn't discuss Shannon with anyone, except maybe Pete. A man didn't like to talk about his failures. "She was petite, blond, cute as a button, and liked any man who would scratch her itch."

"Oh." Well, Beck told herself, what did you expect? You asked him for honesty and he gave it to you. So what's your comeback to that one, Miss Psychologist?

"Some women are like that," he added.

"It must have hurt terribly if you loved her." *Of course he'd love her, you idiot,* Beck thought. A man like Quent wouldn't have married a woman he didn't love.

Quent placed his hand on Beck's neck, his thumb stroking her chin. "Look, Doc, I don't love her anymore. I don't even hate her. She wasn't a one-man woman, and unfortunately I didn't find out that little fact until it was too late."

"I'm sorry."

"Yeah, well, don't waste your sympathy on me. It happened a long time ago, I learned my lesson, and I'm a wiser man."

"Don't you ever intend to marry again?" Beck felt a trembling flow through her body when Quent's fingers moved down her throat, slipped inside the bathrobe and caressed her collarbone.

"I've never thought about it. Maybe. Someday." God, she felt good. Soft, warm, satiny, female flesh.

"Quent?" She cuddled against him.

"Hmmm?" He took her in his arms, pressing her breasts against his chest.

"Did your ex-wife have anything to do with your estrangement from your brother?" She felt him tense the moment she spoke.

Well, buddy boy, do you tell her the truth or do you lie? Quent had been doing a lot of thinking—about Shannon, about Phillip, and about what had happened nearly seven years ago. He'd hated his kid brother, had blamed him instead of Shannon, but long after Phillip had disappeared, Quent admitted the truth. His brother had been one more of Shannon's victims.

"If Phillip and your ex-wife were involved, it would explain why you two didn't stay in touch." Beck knew, without Quent replying, that she'd guessed correctly. What had it done to a strong, macho guy like Quent to find out his younger brother was his wife's lover?

"I didn't know Shannon had been fooling around the entire three years we were married." Quent withdrew from Beck. He laid his head back against the headboard, a look of painful meditation on his face.

She watched his eyes, those incredible blue eyes. He was a beautiful man—*man* being the operative word. Nothing about him was effeminate. From the top of his thick brown hair to the tips of his size-twelve shoes, Quent Yerby was all man.

Suddenly she felt much too warm. Tingling sensations flowed through her body like water seeping down into the roots of a thirsty plant. If only she wasn't afraid. As much as she trusted Quent Yerby, as gentle, kind and understanding as he'd been with her and Josh, he was still a very big, very strong man with the ability to cause her pain. Even though her mind told her how ridiculous the idea was, her emotions couldn't forget the past. Her father's cruelty had left her scarred, and even though she felt the stirrings of desire, those scars dampened the spark of passion.

She wanted to touch Quent, but she didn't. He was back in his own painful past, reliving the betrayal of two people he'd loved. Beck wanted to comfort him, to console him, but her own grief restricted her.

"I suppose we all have our secret pain," Beck said. "I keep hoping that Josh will be able to overcome the horrors he's lived through. When I think how close we came to—"

Quent grabbed her, shutting off her frightened words with his lips. The force of his kiss took her by surprise, leaving her helpless to resist the piercing intensity of his tongue. She melted into his embrace, allowing his big hands to roam freely over her shoulders and ease the robe downward until she felt the belt give way and her breasts brush against his shirt.

She tried to pull away, but he restrained her, one hand clutching the back of her head, the other reaching down to encompass a swelling breast. He continued the kiss, ravishing her mouth, nipping at her lips, unable to disguise the power of his desire.

Passion and fear warred within Beck. She wanted Quent, and yet she feared him, his manly strength. Shoving as hard as she could against him, Beck managed to break her mouth free from his. "Quent, please..."

He kissed her neck and buried his head against her shoulder. "Sorry."

"Oh, Quent," she whispered. She was as sorry as he. She wished she could allow herself the pleasure of sharing sex with Quent. But even if they loved each other, she was uncertain she could trust him enough to give herself freely. He'd asked if she trusted him, and she'd said she did. But she didn't. Not emotionally.

He pulled the lapels of the open robe together, covering the tempting mounds of her high, full breasts. Like a lost and lonely child in need of comfort, he laid his head in her lap, and she caressed the thick, tawny-brown strands of his hair.

"I was supposed to be comforting you," Quent said.

"You were." Her fingertips fondled his ears.

"You were trying to comfort me from a pain that ended years ago, and all I did was try to eat you alive. God, Beck, I need to earn your trust, but I can't stop wanting you."

Her hand stilled on the back of his neck. "I do trust you. At least I trust you more than any man I know, other than Cole. But . . ."

"Whatever happened in your past to make you mistrust men is something you'll have to get over in your own way and your own time. I'm still dealing with my low opinion of women. Finding my brother in bed with my wife sort of soured me on the whole female sex."

Her body tightened, pain and rage wrapping themselves around her, constricting her breathing, tensing her nerves. She felt an intense longing to physically harm Shannon Yerby, wherever she was now. How could any woman loved by Quent want another man? If Quent loved her . . .

"Will you stay with me?" she asked.

Quent sat up, pulled her into his arms, and kissed her tenderly. "Comfort without passion." But the passion was there, suppressed, buried beneath his iron control.

She snuggled into his embrace and they slipped down in the bed. "I need to check on Josh."

"I'll do it later. Get some rest."

They lay there entwined in each other's arms, the sound of nighttime traffic and mournful blues music permeated the cool spring air. Beck's slow, steady breathing let Quent know that she had finally relaxed. As minutes passed, Beck fell into a restful sleep, but Quent lay awake for long hours. He was painfully aroused and needed to escape from temptation, but didn't want to risk disturbing her. So, he held her in his arms while she slept, and for the first time in his life he learned what mutual affection and trust meant between a man and a woman. Rebecca Jane Kendrick had become more important to him than he'd ever wanted her to be. Sooner or later he was going to teach her the meaning of passion, but first he'd have to find a way to erase her fears. When he made love to her, he wanted her eager and responsive—as hot for him as he was for her.

Seven

Beck arranged the crisp vegetables on a tray and set the dip in the middle. Quent's eating habits were atrocious, and she could well imagine how he'd turn up his nose at the colorful carrots, broccoli and cauliflower. The man seemed to exist on a diet of pizza, hamburgers and jelly doughnuts. She had pointed out that, as the man of the house, he needed to set a good example for Josh, and he'd told her that he didn't blame his nephew for refusing to eat things he couldn't even pronounce. So much for her culinary masterpieces. Now she was trying plain, healthy foods. Simple things. Since Elise and Pete were joining them for lunch, she had agreed to fry chicken.

Instead of worrying about minor problems, Beck knew she should be grateful that Josh was beginning to recover from their ordeal in the parking deck almost two weeks ago. The first few days had been the most difficult. Josh hadn't wanted her or Quent out of his sight, and he still refused to return to play-school. One of them was with him at all times. Quent kept Josh with him in the gym almost every day, and the two Yerby males had persuaded Beck to join them each night for a swim after The Jungle closed.

Although Beck's greatest concern had been helping Josh cope, she, too, struggled through each day. There was the ever-present fear that Royce Paxton would find them. And she had to deal with the new and unnerving emotions Quent Yerby had unleashed within her the night he'd held her in his arms while she slept—the night he had proved she could trust him—the night she began to believe it was possible for a big and powerful man to give comfort instead of pain. Quent epitomized everything she'd always feared, and now she found herself irresistibly drawn to him, to the very strength and virility she'd hated for as long as she could remember—since the first time Travis Kendrick had beaten her.

If Quent had taken advantage of her vulnerability, she wasn't sure how she would have handled the situation. She'd been so afraid he would ask more of her than she was prepared to give. But he hadn't pressed her, instead he'd acted as if nothing had changed between them. In the past two weeks, Quent had been protective, caring, bossy, infuriating and, much to her aggravation, he continued calling her "sweet thing."

Beck heard deep-throated laughter and childish giggles coming from outside the apartment seconds before the sound of a key being inserted in the lock alerted her that *her men* were home. Man and boy entered the living room, their bodies damp with sweat, their hair plastered to their heads, and towels draped around their necks.

Quent reached down and swung Josh up in his arms and set the boy securely on his shoulders. Josh grabbed his uncle by the ears and rested his chin on the top of the big man's head.

"What's for lunch, woman?" Quent asked, galloping through the living room, balancing his precious burden on his huge shoulders.

"Fried chicken," Beck announced as she uncovered the lid on the boiling potatoes. "And mashed potatoes."

Quent opened the refrigerator, retrieved a carton of milk, opened it and put it to his mouth.

Beck cleared her throat and eyed him with disapproval. Holding the milk carton inches from his lips, Quent hesitated, then set the carton down on the table. "Come on, pal. Let's get some glasses for our milk."

"Why do we need glasses, Uncle Quent?" Josh asked. "You never use one."

Quent saw Beck smiling triumphantly, as if to say I told you so. "Well, Josh, old buddy, doing things the civilized way is one of the prices we men have to pay to keep a woman in our lives."

Beck couldn't suppress a chuckle. She took two glasses down from the shelf, picked up the milk carton and poured the cold white liquid. "Here," she said, handing Quent a glass. She reached up and pulled Josh into her arms and set him down at the table.

"I guess drinking out of a glass is worth it to keep Beck," Josh said.

Quent ruffled the child's blond curls, swatted Beck playfully on her behind, and sat down beside Josh. "Keeping Beck would be worth just about anything." He tilted the glass and gulped down the milk.

Beck ignored the playful swat and tried to pretend she hadn't heard what he'd said. She didn't dare allow herself to think he could have meant the words he'd spoken. Did he really think keeping her was worth anything? Had she become that important to him?

"Can I have some cookies?" Josh asked.

Beck turned over the chicken pieces frying in the skillet. "Absolutely not. Lunch will be ready soon."

"How soon?" Josh asked.

"As soon as—" Loud knocking at the door interrupted Beck's reply.

Josh jumped up and ran out of the kitchen. "It's Pete."

"Wait Josh," Beck cautioned.

Quent stood and placed his hand on Beck's shoulder. "Give him a chance to do it right. Besides, Pete promised to bring him a candy bar."

Quent and Beck watched as Josh stopped directly in front of the door. "Who's there?" the child asked.

"It's your old buddy Pete, and Ms. Zimmerman," Pete Harris said.

Josh turned to Quent for approval. "Is it all right, Uncle Quent?"

"Yeah, it's all right."

An hour later Beck and Elise shared the cleanup duties. The three males, in typical masculine fashion, had made a hasty retreat to the living room.

"You need a dishwasher," Elise said as she picked up a plate from the drain board and began wiping it.

"A dishwasher is the least of my worries," Beck said, running the scouring pad over the skillet. "There's only so much that can be done with this kitchen."

"You've done a great job with the kitchen and this whole apartment. It doesn't even look like the same place. Quent should be grateful that when you go, you'll be leaving him with a newly decorated home."

Beck didn't want to think about the day she and Josh would be leaving. Even though she longed to see Royce Paxton behind bars, she couldn't bear the thought of losing Quent.

"Hmm, so that's how it is," Elise said. "I can tell by the expression on your face that you're thinking twice about leaving a certain someone."

Elise's voice brought Beck out of her solitary thoughts. "What are you talking about?"

"I'm talking about that gorgeous man in there." Elise nodded her head toward the living room where Quent and Josh sat on the floor playing with Matchbox cars while Pete relaxed on the couch and enjoyed his cigar.

"I didn't know you found Pete attractive," Beck teased.

"Very funny. You know darn well I was referring to Quent. You can't fool me. You've fallen for the guy, haven't you?"

"Don't be silly." Beck placed the last pan in the drain board.

"Hey, no need to deny it. Besides, it looks like the feeling's mutual."

Beck pulled the plug, allowing the water to drain from the sink. "I don't know what's wrong with me, Elise. Quent is the same man I met and disliked that first day at The Jungle, and yet he's different. He's so much more."

"I've been trying to tell you for years that all macho men aren't jerks. Quent Yerby is a real man." Elise placed the dish towel over the remaining pots and pans.

"Am I supposed to know what you mean by that?"

Elise took Beck by the shoulders and marched her to the doorway. "Take a good look and tell me what you see?"

Beck saw Quent down on all fours, crawling around the living room beside Josh as the two of them made engine noises while pushing their miniature automobiles over the wooden floor. Tears burned Beck's throat and stung her eyes. "I see a real man," she said.

Pete looked up and smiled at the two women standing in the kitchen doorway. "That was a mighty fine lunch, Beck.

Even them raw vegetables weren't bad with enough of that dip on 'em.''

"Why thank you, Pete." Beck and Elise walked through the living room. "I'm going to show Elise what I've done with the other bedroom, then I'll be back to help you with your bath, young man."

"Do I have to take a bath?" Josh whined.

"We're going to the zoo this afternoon, remember?" Beck reminded him.

"Hey, I'll make sure he showers and shaves before I do," Quent said.

Josh looked at his uncle, who was at his eye-level on the floor. Quent grinned, and Josh laughed. "Yeah, I'll shower and shave first, Beck."

"Sounds good to me, guys." Beck walked hurriedly into the bedroom, Elise directly behind her. If she didn't escape, she'd cry. She'd never believed in miracles, not even small ones, but she did now. Quent was a miracle. He had changed her life and Josh's forever.

"I used to have to let your dad shower and shave before I did," Quent said. "I was a pretty big guy when Phillip was about your age."

"You were my daddy's big brother, right?" Josh asked.

"Right."

"You liked him, too, didn't you? The same as you like me." Josh looked at Quent with trusting eyes.

"Yeah, I liked your dad. We had a lot of fun together. We—"

"Hey, Josh, did I ever tell you about the time your daddy got his nose broke, down at the gym?" Pete asked.

Quent was thankful that Pete had plunged right into the conversation. He'd been forcing himself to talk about Phillip because Josh wanted to know about his father. But talking about Phillip brought back too many memories, the good and the bad. He'd liked Phillip. Hell, he'd loved him.

After all, they were brothers. Even though Quent had gotten tired of hauling his baby brother out of one mess after another, he'd never stopped loving him, until...

Josh's happy laughter filled the room. Quent didn't want his nephew to know the truth about his father—at least not until he was old enough to ask questions and accept the answers.

"Can I have my candy bar now?" Josh asked Pete.

"Got it right here," Pete said, pulling a huge chocolate bar out of his shirt pocket.

Within minutes, the candy bar had disappeared, all except dark brown smudges around Josh's mouth and the gooey sweetness that clung to the child's fingertips.

"I think it's time for that bath," Quent said. "I'll let you use my razor to shave off that chocolate mustache before Beck sees it."

Josh snuggled close to Quent where they sat on the floor, their backs braced against a chair. "Beck fusses at Pete for bringing me candy bars, but she lets me eat them anyway. Women sure are funny, aren't they, Uncle Quent?"

Out of the mouths of babes, Quent thought. Beck Kendrick was a puzzle he hadn't been able to figure out. He had allowed her to become far too important in his life, and his feelings were bound to lead to trouble. After the night she'd allowed him to hold her in his arms while she slept, he'd thought their personal relationship would become sticky. He'd figured she'd start clinging and making demands and asking what his intentions were. But she didn't. She'd acted as if nothing had happened, so he'd followed her lead. After all, they had more to worry about than their sexual attraction to each other. Royce Paxton was still on the loose and a constant threat to Beck's and Josh's safety. Quent's main concern had to be keeping them out of danger.

* * *

Beck opened the door and flipped on the light switch. Carrying a sleeping Josh in his arms, Quent followed her into the apartment. Twilight stillness shadowed the room as Beck threw her purse on the couch.

She held out her arms. "Here, give him to me, and I'll get him into his pajamas. I can't believe he went to sleep in the middle of touring the zoo."

Quent laughed and looked down at the child in his arms. God, how he'd come to love this little boy. "Why don't you fix me some coffee and yourself some tea, and I'll put Josh to bed."

The phone rang. Beck jumped. "I'll get it," she said.

Quent nodded and headed for his bedroom.

Beck picked up the receiver. "Hello." Hearing only silence, she repeated, "Hello."

Quent stopped at his bedroom door and turned around. "Who is it?" he asked.

"Hello, is someone there?" Beck grasped the phone tightly.

"Take a good look at the kid's stuffed animals," a thick, dark voice said.

"What?" Beck's hand trembled.

"I'm going to do the same thing to you and Josh." Deep, sinister laughs followed his words.

Beck slammed down the receiver. Clutching her arms in a self-protective hug, she closed her eyes and bit down on her lower lip. "Don't take Josh in there. Take him to my bedroom."

"Who was it?" Quent walked toward Beck, a sleeping Josh snuggled against his chest.

"Royce Paxton."

"Damn!"

"He—he knows where we are. He's been here."

"Beck?"

"Please. I'll put Josh in my bed. He can sleep in his clothes." Beck reached out and took Josh from Quent.

"What did Paxton say?"

"He said for us to look at Josh's stuffed animals." She felt her head swimming. Her knees swayed, and she prayed she wouldn't faint.

"He's too heavy for you," Quent said and rushed forward to take Josh. He balanced the tiny body with one arm and slipped the other around Beck.

Together they entered her bedroom. He helped her sit down on the vanity stool beside her dressing table, then jerked back the covers on her bed and settled Josh in the middle, on the bright pink sheets. The child wiggled restlessly for a few seconds, then cuddled peacefully against a huge feather pillow.

Quent moved toward Beck who stared blankly at him. He knew she didn't see him, and suspected that all she could envision was Royce Paxton's face. Quent knelt down and took her by the shoulders. "Beck." When she didn't respond, he shook her gently. "Beck."

She closed her eyes, then reopened them. "He's done something to Josh's toys. He's been in this apartment." The trembling began in her hands and quickly spread throughout her entire body.

Quent tightened his grip on her shoulders. "Take some deep breaths. Do you hear me? Take some deep breaths."

She obeyed. Still kneeling, he pulled her into his arms. "You stay here and I'll go take a look."

"No!" She clung to him, her fingers biting into the soft cloth of his worn denim jacket.

"Paxton might have been lying. We won't know until I check things out."

"I'll go with you." Beck pushed away from Quent.

He saw the determination in her eyes, and refrained from demanding that she stay here in her bedroom with Josh, safe from whatever sight awaited him in the bedroom he shared with his nephew. "All right. Come on." He helped her to her feet.

Standing outside Quent's bedroom, Beck held her breath when he opened the door. Lamplight from the living room poured over the wreckage that had, only hours earlier, been a newly decorated, immaculate and tidy room. Beck gasped and covered her mouth with her closed fist, her knuckles pressing against her lips.

Quent flipped on the overhead light and stepped inside. The twin beds had been thrashed. Pillows, spreads and mattresses lay topsy-turvey on the floor. Every piece of furniture had been ransacked. Bright red spray paint covered the walls with one clearly written word repeated over and over again. Jill. Jill. Jill.

"Oh, my God," Beck cried. She moved into the room slowly, her eyes searching for Josh's stuffed animals. They, too, were on the floor. Pieces of their slashed heads and bodies littered the wooden surface.

Quent grabbed Beck around the waist and turned her completely around. "Let's get out of here. You've seen enough."

"He was here," she said. "He came into our home. How? How?" Beck gasped for air.

Quent picked her up in his arms and carried her into the living room. She felt the nausea rise to her throat and gladly accepted Quent's gentle touch as he laid her on the couch. "This was bound to happen. Sooner or later Paxton was going to find out where you and Josh were living."

Beck tried to sit up, but Quent gently pushed her back down. "Are you saying that you were expecting something like this?" she asked.

"Yes."

"Why didn't you tell me?"

Ignoring her question, he took her hands in his, brought them to his mouth and kissed the top of each. "I've got to call Captain Burgess. Things are going to start happening pretty fast now, and we need to make some plans."

"What . . . what are you talking about?" Once again she tried to sit up, and once again Quent restrained her.

"Will you stop shoving me back down," she yelled. She clutched the front of his shirt and jerked down hard. "Tell me, dammit."

"Paxton isn't acting rationally. Now that he's found you and Josh, he's not going to play a waiting game anymore. My bet is, he'll make another move soon. We need to be ready for him. We need to be one jump ahead of him."

"Quent?"

He ran the back of his hand over her cheek. "I won't let him hurt either of you. Believe me." His eyes pierced her with their intensity.

Beck had never seen Quent look so dangerous, so overwhelmingly predatory. It frightened her, that aura of masculine power, that untamed protective instinct rising to the surface to possess this gentle, caring man she'd grown to trust so completely.

"What . . . what will we do?" she asked.

"Whatever it takes."

Quent closed the door behind Captain Burgess. Dammit to hell, what a night! Regardless of what lay ahead, he wished he could give Beck the reassurances she so badly needed. But he couldn't. If he did, he'd be lying to her, and he knew instinctively she'd eventually despise him for the lie. Decisions had been made. Hard decisions. Some he'd readily agreed to, and others had been forced down his throat. As far as he was concerned, Beck's and Josh's safety was what mattered most, and he'd had to admit that catching Paxton was the only way to assure their safety.

Elise Zimmerman would arrive tomorrow and take Josh away. Although he and Beck knew it was for the best, neither of them could bear the thought of how Josh would react. Even though Quent and Captain Burgess had hatched an almost foolproof plan for getting Josh out of Memphis without Paxton being aware the child was gone, the plan to use Beck as bait to catch the bastard had been agreed to over Quent's strong objections.

Beck walked out of her bedroom, closing the door halfway. Quent turned to face her. "Did you get him back to sleep?"

"Finally." She sat down on the couch and rested her head against the smooth vinyl surface.

"He knows something's wrong." Quent locked and bolted the front door.

"He's a very bright little boy."

Quent moved toward the kitchen. "I think I need one of Pete's beers. Can I get you something?"

"No, thanks. I'll just take a shower and then try to get some sleep." She stood. "Oh, Quent, where are you going to sleep? You couldn't possibly rest in . . . in—"

"I'll make a pallet on the floor in there in the living room," he called out from the kitchen. "Go on and take your shower."

Quent downed two beers. Even though he wasn't overly fond of the taste, he knew their alcoholic content would help him relax. While Beck showered, he dragged a couple of blankets and pillows from his ransacked bedroom and made himself a pallet in the middle of the living room floor.

When she came out of the bathroom, she'd be in need of some tender, loving care, and he figured he was just the man to give her what she needed. He had waited longer for her than he'd ever waited for a woman he wanted. Making love tonight would be good for them both.

Quent removed his jacket and laid it across the back of the couch, then flipped through his selections of tapes until he saw a copy of his favorite Herbie Mann recording. He'd taped it himself off the sixties album, "Stone Flute." Within seconds the tender beat of brushes against a drum and the sensual mixture of flute and piano brought to life the sultry music.

He sat down on the couch, put his feet up on the coffee table, and waited for Beck to emerge from the bathroom. She was a brave lady holding up under such tremendous pressure. Life was damned unfair, placing a woman like Beck and an innocent child in danger of a madman. And starting tomorrow, Beck would be placing herself on the front lines, right in the line of fire. She'd agreed to Burgess's plan to use her as bait to reel in Paxton. Damn! What if something went wrong? What if his promise to keep her safe turned out to be the one promise he couldn't keep?

"Quent?" Beck said.

He looked up and saw her standing beside the couch. Her long, black hair, damp from her shower, hung loosely about her shoulders. Her eyes spoke to him with such soft eloquence, asking for his comfort, pleading for his strength. She wore nothing except his faded blue robe, the one she'd worn two weeks ago when he'd almost made love to her.

He didn't respond verbally. He reached out, took her hands and pulled her down onto his lap. They stared at each other, neither speaking, yet both communicating with the longing in their eyes, the shallow rapid breaths they took, and the gentle touch of their hands still clinging together.

"Quent?"

"I want to make love to you."

"No—I—no..."

"We need each other. Now. Tonight."

"You're afraid," she said, as if suddenly realizing that big, strong men could actually know fear. "You're afraid something might happen to me, that Paxton might get to me without your being able to stop him.''

Quent pulled her into his arms, holding her fiercely, protectively. ''You can change your mind, you know. We can catch Paxton some other way.''

''How?'' she asked, laying her head on Quent's shoulder.

''We'll figure out something.'' He stroked her from her neck to her waist, his touch forceful yet tender.

''No, Quent. Things can't go on like this. I can't live this way, and neither can Josh. If he's ever going to have a normal life, we have to catch Paxton and put him behind bars.''

Quent knew she was right. Soon everything would be resolved, and Beck would be free to go back to her town house and resume her normal life. And Josh could easily become the only link to the woman who was fast becoming the most important thing in his life.

''Can't we try to forget about what lies ahead?'' Beck asked. ''Just for tonight, can't we... can't we just be two people sharing a quiet evening together?''

''You want to play pretend?'' He kissed the side of her neck.

''Yes, perhaps that's what I want. To pretend that there is no danger out there, that you and I are the only two people in the world, that we're safe and happy.''

''The only two people in the world. Sort of like Adam and Eve in the Garden of Eden?''

''Everything always comes down to sex with you, doesn't it?'' Beck jerked away from him, and resisted his attempt to pull her back into his arms.

''What is it with you?'' Damned if he could take much more of this. She kept sending out mixed signals that had him totally confused.

''Me?'' Beck jumped up off the couch. ''What is it with *you?*''

Quent stood up beside her, grabbed her hand and placed it against his arousal. "That's what it is with me, sweet thing. I've got a need I can't get rid of."

Her hand trembled against the zipper of his jeans where his hand covered hers. When she tried to pull away, he pressed her hand harder against him. "You're being vulgar."

He released his hold and she yanked her hand away. "Yeah, I suppose I am. But men get that way sometimes, sweet thing, especially when they're horny."

"Stop calling me sweet thing!"

Quent laughed, the sound a mirthless grunt. "If I had you on your back and was buried deep inside you, you'd *love* hearing me call you sweet thing."

Putting her hands over her ears, Beck moved away from him. She didn't want to hear him talk about making love to her, of being deep inside her. Heaven help her, she'd had too many dreams about it, dreams of loving that had turned into nightmares of a huge man's strength and brutality.

She stopped in the middle of the room, her feet touching the makeshift pallet. Tears filled her eyes. She didn't need this. Not now, not tonight. But she knew this thing between Quent and her had been building for weeks. It was bound to explode sooner or later.

"I want us to be friends. For Josh's sake if for no other reason." She noticed the cautious look on his face, as if he didn't quite trust her, as if he thought she was playing some kind of game. Maybe his ex-wife had done that to him.

"I thought we were friends," he said. "I thought that . . . after all we've been through together, we were more than friends."

She didn't know what to say. He was right, they were more than friends. "We are. It's just that we can't be...I'm not ready for..."

"Tell me you don't want me," he said, moving to stand directly in front of her, but not touching her. "Tell me that I'm imagining this . . . this thing between us. It's desire, you know, sexual desire."

"I've never been able to trust men like you. Big, strong . . . brutal—"

"Brutal? You think I'm brutal?"

"Yes. No. I mean . . ." She turned away and covered her face with her hands.

He eased his arms around her and pulled her back up against his chest. "I could never hurt you."

She trembled. The feel of his powerful body wrapped around her in comfort filled her with overwhelming needs. The need to comfort him. The need to trust him completely. The need to tell him that she loved him. "I know you'd never hurt me. I know it in my mind and my heart, but there's a part of me that's afraid of you. Your past. The way you've spent your life. I know you've killed." She felt him tense and regretted reminding him of something she knew he didn't want to remember.

"What happened to make you so afraid? Who hurt you so badly that you're afraid of men?" Quent held her close, longing to erase the pain she felt.

"My father." She turned in his arms and buried her face in his shoulder, not daring to look at him.

Quent tried to tilt her head up, but she fought against him, burrowing deeper into his shoulder.

"My father was an alcoholic," she said. "He was a Korean war veteran with a lot of physical and emotional scars. My mother died and he found himself alone to raise two children on a disability check. He turned to the bottle more and more. By the time I was six, all I knew was drunken tirades and endless beatings."

Quent's hold on her tightened. He didn't know if he could bear to hear any more. All he could think about was Beck, his Beck, a tiny little girl being brutalized by her own father. "Oh, God, baby."

"He almost beat me to death once." Tears filled her, suffocating her, but none escaped. They were buried deep inside where the pain lived, as vivid and tormenting as it had been so many years ago.

"You don't have to tell me any more," Quent said, lifting her into his arms.

"Quent?"

"I want you. More than I've ever wanted anyone. Trust me. Give me a chance to show you that a man can give pleasure."

"I thought if I was honest with you about my past, you'd understand why—"

He covered her mouth with a sweetly loving kiss. "I want you to stay with me all night, but I don't expect you to make love with me."

Quent lowered her onto the pallet. Her big brown eyes gazed up at him in supplication, and moisture streaked her cheeks. Her mouth opened and her lips trembled. "I...I..." she mumbled.

Quent unbuttoned his shirt, removed it and tossed it on the floor. He pulled off his belt, stepped out of his shoes, took off his socks, and slipped out of his clothes. Beck watched, fascinated by the sight of his near nakedness. He stood there above her wearing nothing but a pair of cotton briefs that did absolutely nothing to hide his arousal.

"Quent?" Her voice quivered.

"I don't sleep in my clothes."

"Oh."

He lay down beside her and pulled her into his arms. How was he going to teach her about passion without frightening her? he wondered. She needed to learn about the pleasure a man could give a woman without worrying about giving anything in return. She trusted him, but not sexually. Tonight he had to prove to her that the trust between them extended to every aspect of their relationship.

"There will be no pain from me. Not ever." He kissed her cheek, nuzzling his nose against the side of her face.

"I dream about you, you know," she admitted.

God! Why had she told him? He had called forth all his reserved strength in order to keep himself from taking her, and now she was telling him that she dreamed about him.

"I dream you're making love to me."

His lips stilled. "I dream about it, too. Awake and asleep, I dream of being inside you, taking you hard and fast and exploding like skyrockets on the Fourth of July."

"But my dreams always turn into nightmares." The look in her eyes said it all. No passion. Only fear. "We're making love, then suddenly you stop loving me. You yell at me and start hitting me. Harder and harder."

He took her head in one big hand and forced her to look at him. "Trust me."

Quent kissed her, a whisper-light kiss. He traced the outline of her lips with his tongue, then anointed her face with kisses as fragile as butterfly wings. His hand tightened in her hair, bringing her face to rest against his. He held her, simply held her, with his heart beating wildly and his manhood throbbing with need.

"I'm going to open the robe and look at you," he said as he gently pushed her down on her back.

"Quent?" She clutched the front of the robe tightly.

He lifted her hand away and loosened the belt. Ever so slowly, he opened the garment to gradually reveal the beauty of her sleek, round body, but allowed himself only a few precious moments to enjoy the sight. "Turn over on your stomach."

She obeyed, and he removed the robe. Her damp hair lay across her naked back. Quent pushed the silky black strands toward her shoulders and lowered his head.

She felt the warmth of his breath on her neck, seconds before his tongue touched her flesh. She jerked. He ran his hand down her back from shoulder to hip.

"Trust me," he whispered.

She gave herself over to him in that moment, knowing she could refuse him nothing. She was entirely at his mercy, but she wasn't afraid. She knew he wouldn't hurt her.

For such a sweet, endless time he worshipped her with his hands and mouth and tongue. She trembled. She sighed. She cried out. And the pleasure went on.

With the upmost care, Quent turned her naked body over so that she faced him. He brought her hand to his mouth and planted a wet kiss in the palm. "You taste so good," he told her. "And you smell like exotic flowers. That's what you've always reminded me of, an elegant exotic flower."

His tongue moved up and down her thumb. One by one he traced the outline of her fingers, leaving a trail of moisture on her delicate flesh.

"Quent . . . Quent . . ."

She was the most beautiful, desirable woman in the world, and he wanted to love her, completely, the way a man and woman are meant to love. But she wasn't ready for his possession. So, tonight he would teach her about pleasure and allow her to possess him.

"Let me give you pleasure." He lowered his head to her breast, took the nipple in his mouth and sucked greedily.

Beck's body bucked up off the pallet. Quent's fingers pinched at the other nipple until she moaned, her hips twisting, her legs writhing. "Noooo . . ." she cried out.

"Yes, baby. Yes."

His tongue painted a wet path from her breasts to the apex of her thighs. When his fingers raked through the black curls and found the vulnerable flesh hidden below, Beck tried to close her legs tightly, but he prized them apart, soothing her with his touch, petting her with his tongue.

"You mustn't," she whimpered.

"You're wrong," he said. "I must."

Beck had never known such an unselfish loving, such an abandoned display of caring. She felt embarrassed and thrilled, wanton and totally female. And then all she could feel was the constant stroking of Quent's tongue, the ceaseless building of sensation in the very core of her body. He took her higher and higher, closer and closer to the edge. She gripped his shoulders seconds before she dropped off the pinnacle and plunged into earth-shattering ecstasy. Her body convulsed into spasms of release so intense she thought she would surely die from the pleasure.

Quent moved upward to lie beside her, pulling her damp body against him. "You're so hot, so very hot."

"Quent?"

"Go to sleep, Rebecca Jane." He hugged her to him. "I just want to hold you."

"But you didn't—"

"Tonight, you possessed me." He kissed her cheek.

She snuggled closer, shut her eyes and kissed his shoulder. Yes, she thought, tonight she had indeed possessed him, and yet, without having invaded her body, without having sought his own release, he had possessed her, her heart and her very soul.

Within minutes Beck slept. Her soft, even breathing told Quent that his loving ministrations had relaxed her physically and mentally. He had given her the fantasy of their being the only two people in the world. But he was wide awake and still throbbing. He'd never made love to a woman without seeking his own satisfaction, but in giving to Beck, he had received a special gift. He had proven himself worthy of her complete trust.

Hours passed and she lay nestled in the security of his arms. During those still and timeless moments before dawn, he dozed on and off, waking often to savor the feel of her sweet body as he caressed her. But as the first glimmer of daylight crept into the room, Quent could no longer bear the painful arousal that had tormented him throughout the night. He eased away from Beck and stood up. On his way to the bathroom, he checked on Josh who slept peacefully on pink satin sheets.

Quent turned on the shower, stepped inside and yelped as the ice-cold water hit him.

Eight

The May morning came bright and clear, with all the warmth of springtime sunshine, a blue sky and a breeze so light it merely caressed the treetops. Beck gazed out the living room windows above Overton Square and wondered how this place had come to feel like home in so short a time. Although she missed her town house, she realized that her fancy Germantown apartment had never really been a home. It had been, and was, an elegant statement of Dr. Rebecca Jane Kendrick's wealth and impeccable taste.

Oddly enough Beck's opinion of Midtown had changed as well as her opinion of The Jungle. The building, like most of the square's other structures, reflected its twenties origins. She'd actually enjoyed seeing what she could do with the shambles Quent called an apartment. The rooms above the gym had real potential, and the fun she'd experienced in making minor improvements in Quent's living quarters came from the fact that they'd done the work together. She had wanted to do more than add a few pieces of used furniture, but Quent had been adamant that she spend very little of her own money. *Men! Men and their fragile egos!*

If the threat of Royce Paxton hadn't loomed over them like a giant shadow during the weeks she and Josh had spent with Quent, she would have loved every minute of experiencing life with such a vital man and being exposed, on a firsthand basis, to the variety of aromas, sounds and people of Overton Square. From the Book Cottage to the Boogie Rock Cafe, from Playhouse on the Square Theater to Gonzles and Gertrude's Mexican Cantina, this area had come to mean more to her than just the "in place" for good food, quaint shops and hot nightlife.

But Quent's home and Beck's possessive feelings for both the man and his habitat would mean very little in the next few days. Once Josh was safely out of Memphis, the trap for Paxton would be set, and once Jill's killer was in jail, Beck and Josh would return to Germantown.

After last night, Beck admitted she had no desire to leave Quent. She trusted him in every way. For the first time in her life she knew she was ready to give herself completely to a strong and virile man. She realized now how sensitive Quent was to her emotional needs. In keeping such iron control over his own needs, he'd given Beck a precious gift. By loving her body with such unselfish adoration, he taught her that a big and powerful man could indeed give pleasure instead of pain. Quent Yerby would never hurt her. It wasn't in his nature.

Somehow she'd known that he wouldn't taunt her with the way she'd abandoned herself to his loving, that he wouldn't remind her of the power she'd given him to control her body. His gift had been free, with no strings attached.

But Beck wanted strings. She wanted a commitment. She wanted a lifetime with the man she loved, and she loved

Quent Yerby in a way she'd never known existed...with every breath she took, with every beat of her heart.

Closing the bedroom door, Quent stopped and watched Beck as she stared out the window. He wondered if she was thinking about him, about last night. He walked up behind her, slipped his arms around her and pulled her back against his chest.

"Penny for your thoughts," he whispered in her ear, then placed a quick kiss on her neck.

"Where's Josh?" Beck asked, afraid to tell Quent where her thoughts had traveled.

"He's feeding the turtle his Uncle Pete gave him."

Beck laughed, remembering the look on Josh's face when he and Pete returned from the gym earlier this morning. Pete had taken Josh downstairs to give Quent and Beck a chance to clean up the ransacked bedroom and smear a fresh coat of paint over the walls. Where on earth Pete had gotten "Wally Turtle" Beck didn't even bother to ask. She was simply grateful that Pete had given the boy a pet, something he could take with him when Elise came for him this afternoon.

"I dread telling Josh that he has to leave us." Beck turned, burrowing her head into Quent's shoulder, seeking comfort and finding it.

Soothing her with his gentle touch, Quent kissed the side of her face. "It won't be easy on any of us, least of all Josh, but we've got to get him out of Memphis. For his own safety."

"I know. Oh, God, I know."

They looked at each other, and suddenly it was last night all over again. The hours between simply disappeared. The desire was there, the need, the caring.

"Beck..." Quent's lips hovered over hers, yearning, wanting with a hunger that couldn't be denied.

Their lips met with a gentle pleading that quickly turned wild. Kisses weren't enough, no matter how untamed. Quent's body needed more, and his heart demanded more.

"Hi," Josh said. "Whatcha doing? Kissing?" The child stood by the open bedroom door smiling at the two adults who quickly broke apart, as if they'd been caught doing something illegal.

"Hey, there, pal," Quent said, wondering if he should try to explain to Josh about the kiss, about what was going on between him and Beck. But how could he explain when he wasn't sure himself? He knew he wanted Beck more than he'd ever wanted another woman, and that he felt a deep sense of possessiveness where she was concerned, but how could he say that to his four-year-old nephew?

"You and Beck gonna get married or something?" Josh asked, touching the two adults with his pleading look.

Beck took Josh's hand and walked him around to the sofa where she sat down and pulled him onto her lap. "People kiss for all kinds of reasons, honey. Your Uncle Quent and I like each other. We've become friends, and sometimes... well, sometimes friends kiss each other."

Josh smiled at Beck, then turned his head toward his uncle who still stood by the windows. "You kissed Beck like people do on TV."

Quent came around and sat down on the sofa. "Look, pal, I know you'd like for me and Beck to get together so the three of us could be a real family, but Beck and I aren't ready to get married. Not right now."

"When will you be ready?" Josh slipped off Beck's lap, and placed himself between the two adults.

"Before Quent and I can think about the future, about how the three of us are going to work things out about being a family, we have to take care of other problems." Beck didn't want to frighten Josh, didn't want to remind him that their immediate problem was catching a man who wanted to see them both dead.

"You can't get married until the police get Royce," Josh said.

Beck's heart ached for the maturity in the child's words, the knowledge no four-year-old should have. "Something like that." There was no point in destroying Josh's dream of one big happy family. There would be time enough to deal with that once the present nightmare had ended.

"Then I hope they get him soon." Josh reached out and grabbed Beck's hand and then Quent's. He held tightly, his small fingers clutching fiercely as he pulled both adult hands together, his small one caught between the two larger ones.

Beck swallowed, trying to hold back the tears threatening to surface. This precious child—her little boy—had known so much fear and pain in his short life. More than anything she wanted to give him the love, the care, the stability he longed for and had never had. "The police are going to catch Royce Paxton, and soon. But we have to help them."

Josh's tiny hand trembled slightly, then fell away. Beck released Quent's hand, took Josh's and brought it to her lips. "Don't be afraid, honey. Royce will never get anywhere near you again."

"But we can all help the police get Paxton," Quent said. "You can help." He knew Josh wouldn't want to leave, would fight being taken away from the security he felt with Beck. Somehow they had to find a way to make this separation acceptable to him.

"How can I help?" Josh's little voice quivered.

"You can help by playing a game with us. It's a long, long game. It may last for days, even weeks." Beck hoped that by presenting the inevitable to Josh in a simple childlike way might make the parting less painful.

"What kinda game?" Josh asked, his interest obviously piqued.

"This afternoon Elise is going to bring some children from the shelter to visit Uncle Quent's gym." Beck forced a smile, desperately trying to infuse the idea with elements of fun and adventure.

"The shelter where we...where my mommy and me stayed?" Josh's big blue eyes filled with tears.

"Yes," Beck said. "It's going to be like a party. Uncle Quent's calling it Children's Day at The Jungle. Another lady, a very nice lady will be with Elise." Beck sighed, wishing there was some other way to do this. "The nice lady is a policewoman."

Josh turned his head into Beck's side, hiding his face in the soft cotton of her blouse.

Quent touched Josh's shoulder. "I've known Ms. Brennan a long time. She's taken care of a lot of people, a lot of boys and girls. She likes children. She'll...she'll like you."

Josh burrowed deeper against Beck. She slipped her arms around him and lifted him back into her lap. "During the party this afternoon, Elise is going to help you get dressed up in a costume. Won't that be fun?"

With his head resting on Beck's breast, his tiny body curled into hers, Josh gnawed on his lower lip.

"We're going to let you dress up like a girl, a girl with pigtails," Quent told his nephew. He tried to make his voice sound light and frivolous.

"I don't wanna," Josh whined.

"You want to help the police catch Royce, don't you, honey?" Beck asked, stroking the child's back.

"Uh-huh." Josh closed his eyes and clung to Beck.

"It'll take a big boy to do what we're asking. It won't be easy." Beck hugged him gently.

"What...what do I have to do?" Josh sniffled.

"You've got to go to the party today. You've got to let Elise help you get into your costume, and then, when the other children leave with Elise and Ms. Brennan, you have to go with them."

"No! No! I won't go!" Josh grabbed Beck around the neck, clinging to her as tears ran down his round, chubby face. His big, blue eyes opened wide with sheer panic and his body shook with fear.

Oh, God! Beck cried silently. I knew this was going to happen. And I knew there was nothing I could do to prevent it. She couldn't check the tears burning her eyes. Biting her lip, clenching her teeth and taking several deep breaths couldn't stop the onslaught of emotions that erupted inside her. She could well imagine the enormous agony raging within Josh at this exact moment. If anyone had taken her away from Cole, she would have fought like a demon. Her brother had been her only salvation, the one person who stood between her and the deep, dark abyss of being alone.

"It'll only be for a little while." Beck's voice cracked. She swallowed back the tears and felt them choking her. She had to keep control. For Josh's sake.

"Please, Beck, don't make me go away." His tiny fingers pinched at the cottony fabric of Beck's blouse. "Please. Please. I'll be good. I'll be so good."

What little was left of her professional objectivity disappeared as she held Josh in her arms and allowed herself to cry freely. "Oh, baby. My sweet, sweet baby."

Why, dear Lord? Why? Help me. Help Josh. Help us all get through this, she prayed. If they allowed him to stay, there was no way they could be one hundred percent sure they could keep him safe, and yet, if they sent him away, would he ever recover from the separation?

Beck looked over at Quent, her soft brown eyes beseeching him, begging for an alternative solution when she knew there was none. "Quent?"

When he tried to touch Josh, the child shivered and clung to Beck all the more. "Josh. I want you to listen to me."

Beck breathed in her tears. Her chest ached. Her head throbbed. And her heart began to break. "You'll always be my little boy. My little boy and Uncle Quent's."

"We're not going to leave you," Quent said, his big hand resting on Josh's back. "This is just a little trip. When the police have Paxton in jail, you can come home, and then you'll never have to go away again."

"No. Please don't make me leave." Josh's little hand patted Beck's cheek. "Please, Beck. I love you."

She sucked in her breath and caught the onslaught of fresh tears. The pain inside her grew and grew and grew. Like a giant tumor, it expanded until it threatened her very existence. "I love you, too, baby. So much."

"If you stay here in Memphis, Royce Paxton might be able to get to you. He might be able to hurt you." Quent hated himself for being so blunt, but he decided it might well be the only way to get through to his nephew.

Beck's face tightened with condemnation, and she shook her head quickly in a negative response. "Quent," she whispered disapprovingly.

"Beck and I love you," Quent said. "Once this is over, we're going to find a way to be a family. I'm going to be your father, and Beck's going to be your mother. Both of us are going to be here for you from now on. But right now, we want you out of danger. The only way we can keep you safe is to send you away."

Josh held tightly to Beck's neck, but he turned his head slightly in order to look at his uncle. "You could take care of me. You won't let Royce hurt me if I stay here."

"I wish I could promise you that, but I can't." Quent had never felt so impotent, so totally useless in his entire life. He was helpless against the truth, and the truth was that he couldn't take care of his own.

"Uncle Quent is going to take care of me while I help the police catch Royce," Beck said, finally able to regain some control over her emotions. "If Quent's trying to take care of you, too, Royce might get away. And you don't want that to happen, do you, honey?"

"No. I—I don't want Royce to hurt you the way he did Mommy. I don't want him to hurt anybody. Not ever, ever again." Although his face was tear-stained and his eyes were still damp, Josh didn't cry as he looked squarely at Quent. "Promise . . . promise I can come back?"

Quent felt the blow to his chest as if he'd collided with a Mack truck. He'd never known such pain, and prayed he'd never experience it again. "Hey, you're my little boy, aren't you? There's no way you're going to get rid of me, no matter what."

"We promise," Beck pledged, her heart beating rapidly, her whole being filled with a mixture of relief and dread. "We promise you'll be home with us soon."

"You're going to be my new mommy?" Josh asked.

"Yes, honey." She wanted to say more, but couldn't. If she said another word, she'd cry again.

"And Uncle Quent's going to be my daddy?"

"You bet I am." Quent put his arms around Beck, and pulled her and Josh into his embrace. Somehow, someway, the three of them were going to live through this nightmare. And when it was all over, they would have to find a way to give Josh the kind of life he deserved.

After adjusting the volume on the battered old radio, Quent leaned back in the swivel chair at his desk, rested his feet on an open bottom drawer and tried to relax while listening to WEVL. He'd left Beck and Josh outside, in The Jungle, to spend the last precious moments together before Josh would be taken away—taken out of danger and into safekeeping.

Perhaps he'd come in here to brood, to try to digest the fact that their fate was out of his hands. He had a woman and a child who meant everything to him, and yet he didn't possess the power to protect them without outside help. Admitting that truth dented his male pride just a bit. He didn't like the idea that Beck would be putting her life on the line in order to catch a killer.

While Burgess set the trap for Paxton, Josh would be safe. Quent knew his old friend Russ Sellers and his wife, Janet, would provide a safe place for Josh to stay. Russ was an ex-soldier and former Memphis cop who'd married and settled down in a sleepy Mississippi town where he was now the police chief.

If only they could send Beck somewhere just as safe. But she was determined to help Burgess catch Paxton, and tomorrow the police would put their plan into action.

Quent had tried not to let himself think beyond the next few days, beyond the present danger, but he couldn't control the way his thoughts kept moving into the future. In the years since his divorce from Shannon, he certainly hadn't lived like a monk, but he'd never once gotten serious about a woman. These powerful feelings he had for Beck bothered him. He could handle the fact that he wanted her, he could even accept the fact that he'd grown to like and respect her, but he didn't want to admit that there was more to their relationship. A man didn't feel as possessive and protective of a woman as he did Rebecca Jane Kendrick unless he loved her, but Quent wasn't ready for love. Hell, he didn't want to love Beck. She was the type of woman who'd want a wedding band and a lifetime commitment, and he wasn't sure he was willing to put his head in that noose again.

Quent jumped to his feet, ran his hand over his jawline and rubbed the back of his neck. Damn, he hated this whole mess! He didn't want to have to send Josh away, and the very thought of putting Beck in danger sent boiling hot fury through him.

Pacing around the tiny, dim office, Quent felt trapped not only by the confines of the small space but by his own unchecked emotions. If only there was some way he could get to Paxton, he'd make sure the man never hurt another living soul. Men capable of abusing women and children were little more than wild animals, and despite people like Beck who preached forgiveness and rehabilitation, Quent wondered if the best method of prevention wasn't annihilation. *Well, old pal, that kind of thinking would get you nowhere with Beck. She can't understand or accept the need for physical violence.* Hell, maybe she was right.

Quent flung open the office door and moved along the corridor toward the weight room where Children's Day was in full swing. A dozen children of various sizes, ages and sexes romped around The Jungle. One tiny boy hung about Pete's shoulders like a little monkey attached to his mother's back. A freckle-faced redhead clung to a cluster of multicolored balloons, her yellow-green eyes riveted to the big blond man lifting weights.

In the corner of the room, Josh stood silently as Beck adjusted the pigtails attached to his wig. *They look so right together,* Quent thought, as he watched his nephew and the very motherly woman trying so hard to reassure him.

Dear God, but she was beautiful. So beautiful. Every soft, satiny inch. From the creamy flesh of her shoulders to the rounded curve of her breasts, Beck was perfection. From her tiny waist to her luscious legs, she was flawless.

As long as he lived he'd never forget the look of her lying before him totally naked, completely trusting. Last night he had memorized the taste and smell of her, so pure and sweet and unlike anything he'd ever known. Forever etched on his fingertips was the warm, silky feel of her body as she lay in his arms. The sound of her orgasmic moans and cries reverberated in the secret recesses of his heart.

Today, she was still the same woman, his gloriously responsive Beck, but she was different, too. She was her usual stylish, proper self dressed in burgundy linen slacks and mauve silk blouse. Her trademark diamond studs adorned her ears and a hand-tooled silver bracelet circled her wrist. Forever the lady, he thought, always striving for complete control.

Quent walked into the room. His presence caught her attention immediately. She smiled and waved. Quent could see Josh stiffen at her side, as if he thought his uncle's appearance meant the moment for goodbye had arrived.

Quent stopped directly beside Beck, but didn't touch her or Josh. If he touched either of them, he'd probably drag them into his arms and never let them go. Better to refrain from stupidity at this point. No sense making a fool of himself.

"Ms. Brennan is going to take you straight to Uncle Quent's friend's house," Beck said. "Russ and Janet Sellers are very nice people, and they're going to take good care of you." She knew Josh would be safe miles away in Mississippi with Quent's old army buddy and his wife and their three children, but she dreaded the separation almost as much as Josh did.

"They got a big old house on a farm," Josh said, pulling on the hem of his pink shorts. "And three kids for me to play with."

"You'll like the farm, all those pigs and cows and chickens." Please, God, Beck prayed, don't make this too difficult for him. He's such a little boy and he's been hurt so much. Keep him safe until he can come home to us.

"Come get me soon." Josh threw his arms around Beck's neck and hugged tightly.

"Very soon," was all she could say.

Ms. Brennan, a tall, slender woman in her mid-forties, placed her hand on Josh's shoulder. "Ms. Zimmerman is gathering up the other children. It's time for us to go."

"Beck!" Josh clung tenaciously, his hands gripping Beck's arms.

Quent knelt down beside Josh, but didn't touch him. "If you're going to help us catch Royce Paxton, you have to go with Ms. Brennan."

Slowly, hesitantly, Josh released his hold on Beck and took Ms. Brennan's outstretched hand. Obviously trying not to cry, he puckered his lips and shook his head affirmatively. His big blue eyes, so like Quent's, filled with tears.

"We're very proud of you," Quent said.

With easy steps, Ms. Brennan began walking Josh toward the bevy of children congregated with Elise at the front entrance. Just as they reached the exit, Josh turned and looked back at Quent and Beck. He raised one little hand and waved.

"We love you," Beck said, but wasn't sure Josh could hear her above the noise of the gym and the clattering excitement of Elise's energetic brood.

The front door opened, thirteen children and two adults walked out, and the door closed. Beck stood, her eyes locked on the emptiness. It took all her willpower not to run outside, grab Josh and keep him with her.

Quent walked over to Beck, wanting to take her in his arms. Noting the tenseness, the abject loneliness he saw surrounding her, he decided against it. "He'll be all right."

"Will he?" Beck didn't even look at Quent. She turned quickly and fled.

"Beck!"

Should he go after her or should he leave her alone? Quent wondered. She had headed straight for the stairs leading up to the apartment. She hadn't turned to him for comfort, hadn't asked him to share her pain.

"Captain Burgess is on the phone," Pete Harris said. "I guess he's eager to set the trap for Paxton, huh?"

"Yeah. We're putting things in motion tomorrow."

"You don't like the idea of using Beck as bait, do you?"

"Damn right I don't."

"It's the only way."

"It's the quickest, easiest way."

"She's got guts, our lady doc."

Quent didn't reply. He didn't want to think about his gutsy Rebecca Jane being in danger. And she was his, make no mistake about that. If Royce Paxton harmed one hair on her head, he'd pay dearly. Quent knew Beck would hate the thought of revenge. She was gentle, kind, loving. His violent past was a part of him that she had a hard time accepting. He wondered how she'd react if he told her Captain Burgess was pressuring him to return to the force.

Nine

Beck looked down at her hands and toyed with the tips of her long, tapered nails, then twisted the ruby-and-diamond ring on her right index finger. With her hip hugging the armrest and her head propped up against the back edge of the sofa, she reached out for a throw pillow and clutched it to her breast. The tears had stopped hours ago, replaced with the chilling numbness that protected her from any more pain. Josh was gone, and she'd had no choice but to let him leave. She couldn't help wondering if he would recover from this separation.

Threatening dark clouds replaced the sunshine as afternoon turned to evening. Dingy gray light fell across the living room, casting somber shadows on the walls and floor, across the furniture, over Beck's still body. Thunder echoed in the distance, the trumpeting sound blending smoothly with the bluesy rhythm of Grover Washington, Jr.'s "Masterpiece" playing on the stereo.

Rebecca Jane Kendrick hadn't felt so alone and so afraid since she'd been a child, since the last time her father had beaten her. In the years since Cole had taken her away and eventually given her everything money could buy, she had fought valiantly to overcome the tormenting memories of her past. She had chosen her profession not only to help others like herself, but in the hope of freeing herself from the debilitating fears that chained her to yesterday.

She could feel the past closing in around her, as it did occasionally. But this time was different. It wasn't just her own past that threatened to suffocate her, but Quent's past and her precious little Josh's. Did she have the strength it would take to unite the three of them and keep them together forever? Could she help Josh overcome the brutality he'd lived through when she had never totally escaped her own childhood nightmares? Was she woman enough to capture a man like Quent Yerby and possess him completely?

Beck sat up and leaned over, resting her elbows on her knees while burying her face in the soft pillow clutched in her arms. *Oh, Quent, I need you. I need you so badly,* her heart cried. But he wasn't here. She was all alone in the apartment, alone with the past, with her fears and uncertainties.

In the hours since Elise and Ms. Brennan had taken the children away, Beck had brooded alone while Quent stayed downstairs at The Jungle. Perhaps he didn't need her the way she needed him. Perhaps he thought she wanted to be alone because she'd run away from him. More than likely, he simply didn't want to have to contend with a weepy, half-hysterical woman. Typical macho men didn't like to deal with overly emotional females. But Quent wasn't a typical macho man, she reminded herself. He was loving and gentle and understanding.

Then why isn't he here with you now when you need him so badly? she asked herself. *If you want him, go get him.*

Just get up, walk downstairs and throw yourself into his arms.

No. She couldn't do that. She'd wait. Surely, sooner or later, he'd come to her.

The deafening roar of thunder shook the room, and a slash of brilliant lightning streaked through the windows, momentarily vanquishing the dreary gloom. The pillow fell to the floor as Beck stood up and focused her gaze on the world outside and the tender new raindrops just beginning to fall. A life-giving springtime thunderstorm developed as Beck stood looking out along Overton Square.

Low and dark and melancholy, the hypnotizing strands of a saxophone encircled Beck as the music flowed from the stereo. *Alone, alone, alone,* the moody, sweet tune seemed to murmur. *Unloved, unloved, unloved,* the heavy, languid beat of the rain seemed to cry.

Mindless with pain and need, Beck turned and ran out of the apartment and down the back stairs. Wanting only to escape the tormenting melody playing in her mind, Beck ran down the hallway, unheeding of Quent when he called out to her. *Escape. Escape.* She had to escape the pain, the hunger.

Beck flung open the back door to the alley parking area and, not hearing Quent's insistent yells, she ran outside into the downpour.

Quent walked to the doorway, stopped, and watched Beck standing near her car, the rain drenching her as flashes of lightning streaked the sky. What the hell was the matter with her? he wondered. Was she planning on going somewhere in her car? Had something happened upstairs that frightened her? Why had she run past him instead of coming to him?

"Beck," he called out, but the thunder muffled the sound of his voice.

With her head held high, she stood silently while raindrops covered her upturned face, plastered her long black hair to her head and turned her blouse transparent. The look on her face frightened him, that soulful, lost look of a child close to tears.

Quent rushed through the heavy deluge and grabbed Beck by the shoulders. She stiffened, her back rigid, her eyes glazed and unseeing. "Beck?" When she didn't respond, he shook her gently. "Honey, what are you doing out here?"

"It's raining," she said as if in answer to his question, a blank expression on her face.

"Yes, it's raining. We need to go inside. Where'd you think you were going?" He put his arm about her waist and tried to turn her. She stood, tense and unmoving.

Slowly she reached out and touched his damp face. "You're getting wet."

Dammit, he didn't like this. He didn't like it one little bit. She was acting weird, and he wasn't sure how to handle the situation. He pulled her against him and once again tried to get her to move forward. She wouldn't budge. "Beck, let's go inside."

"I can't. Oh, please, Quent, I can't." She fell into his arms, hugging him fiercely. "Help me. Help me."

"What do you want me to do?" If she asked him to lie down and die for her, he would. He'd do anything she asked.

"Make it go away. Please make it go away." Still clinging to him, with her arms wrapped around his waist, she threw her head back and gazed up into his face.

"Make what go away?" He realized she was fighting some unseen demon, some monster from deep within her soul.

"The pain. Make the pain go away."

Oh, God! Her words brought her pain to life for him. It delved inside him and took hold. Her pain was his, for now and forever, and only together would they ever be able to appease the agony. "I can feel it, Beck, but I'm stronger. Together, we're stronger. I'll help you fight it."

He picked her up and carried her inside. Pete stood by the doorway, a look of concern on his grizzly old face.

"She going to be all right?" Pete asked.

"Damn right she is," Quent snapped as he headed for the back staircase.

He took the stairs two at a time, carrying his precious burden up to the second-floor apartment. The front door stood open, the last dim light of day casting a dusky glow over the room.

The woman in his arms clung to him, her wet clothes sticking to his. He carried her inside and eased her down onto the couch. She held on to him tenaciously, her arms tightening around his neck. He reached up and tried to free himself, but she refused to release him.

"It's all right, Beck. I won't leave you."

Still clinging to him, she shook her head. "You left me alone up here all afternoon. I needed you."

Dammit to hell! He had deliberately allowed her the time alone he thought she needed. When she'd run out of the gym and away from him, he'd assumed she didn't want to be disturbed. He'd fought against the urge to come upstairs and check on her, but he'd been so sure she wanted to be alone. He'd been mistaken, badly mistaken. The last thing on earth she'd needed was to be alone.

"I'm here now. Everything's going to be all right." He eased her hands from around his neck. "We need to get out of our wet clothes."

Beck looked at him and actually saw him. His jeans and short-sleeved shirt were soaking, his hair was plastered to his head, and rainwater moistened his face. "Oh, Quent. I . . . I didn't mean for this to . . . I . . ."

"Talk to me, Beck. Tell me what happened while you were up here all alone." He reached out and began unbuttoning her blouse.

She allowed him the intimacy, not once flinching as he removed her wet blouse. "I couldn't stop thinking about Josh. About how scared he was. I kept hearing him beg us not to send him away."

"He'll be all right. We made him understand why he had to go, and he knows he'll be coming home as soon as possible." Quent unsnapped his Western shirt, slipped out of it and threw it on the floor atop Beck's blouse.

"And then I started remembering." She stood up, her eyes bright and clear, without one single tear. "I remembered all the times he'd hit me. All the times I'd cried and begged him to stop. And when Cole tried to help me, he'd hit him, too."

Quent stood and took her in his arms, kissing her face over and over again, the gesture one of loving concern. "No one will ever hurt you again. I promise."

"Royce Paxton could get to me before you could stop him. We both know that."

"You don't have to go through with this. We can find another way." He ran his hands up and down her limp arms.

"It has to end soon. None of us can take much more. Having to leave us could well be the final straw for Josh. My nerves are shot to hell. I've let all my old pain and fear drive me to acting irrationally. And you. God, Quent, you've put your entire life on hold for Josh and me."

He took her chin in his big hand and forced her to look at him. "Don't you understand that you and Josh have become my life?" He hadn't meant to say that, wasn't even sure where the words had come from, but, by God, he meant them.

Beck jerked away, turning her back to him as she clutched her body in a tight hugging motion. She knew what she wanted, what she needed more than she'd ever needed anything in her life. She needed Quent Yerby. She needed him with her, around her, inside her. No matter what happened tomorrow or the day after, she wanted him tonight. She saw so clearly that he was the one person who could ease the pain forever, the one man who could take away the bitter loneliness.

For as long as she could remember she'd been afraid of large, virile men with deep voices and big hands. She had shied away from blatantly masculine males, dating only the most timid, tame specimens she could find. Sex held little meaning for her. She had never known passion, had never felt desire. Not until Quent Yerby entered her life and made her feel things she'd never imagined herself capable of feeling.

With her future balanced on a fine line, with death a real possibility, Beck wanted to experience the full richness of life, and she knew she could achieve that goal only with Quent Yerby. He alone could take her to her desired destination—to complete fulfillment as a woman.

With the low, sexy sound of Miles Davis's trumpet saturating the room with his steamy rendition of "Summertime," Beck turned and looked at Quent. He stood perfectly still, watching her with those blue eyes. Slowly, seductively, she unzipped her wet linen slacks and slid them downward, then kicked them aside. Standing before him in nothing but her mauve bikini panties and sheer lacy bra, Beck wet her lips with the tip of her tongue, arched her neck and ran her fingers through the damp strands of her silky hair. She was acting on sheer instinct—primitive female instinct that guided her body on its seductive quest.

He watched as she moved toward him, each step a slow, deliberate torment. His whole body tensed with the pain of arousal, and his manhood pulsed with throbbing need against his tight jeans.

She stopped directly in front of him, her eyes warm and inviting, her lips wet and open, her body flushed, her pebble-hard nipples jutting against their lacy restraints.

"Do you have any idea what you're asking for?" His voice was a husky male growl.

The stereo music changed to a jazzy Latin rhythm, the drumbeat matching the accelerating strum of Beck's heart. "I want to know what it's like," she admitted. Taking a deep breath, she reached out and touched his naked chest. "I have to know."

"Don't tease me, lady. Don't say anything you don't mean." He could feel the heat of her slender hand where it rested on his hairy chest, her very touch burning him.

"I've always been afraid to trust myself, to... to allow myself..."

He slipped his arm around her. "Are you trying to tell me that you want me?"

"You're so big and so very strong. You could easily hurt me." She maneuvered her hand through his chest hair allowing the curly strands to wrap around her fingers.

"Haven't I proven that you can trust me?" He clutched her elbows and jerked her forward, capturing her hands between them.

"Will you make love to me, Quent? Please."

"Will I..." He grabbed the back of her head and pulled her mouth up to his. Forgetting tenderness and control, acting only on the passion, the raging hunger driving him insane, Quent took her mouth, thrusting inside like a predator claiming his captured prey. His other hand slid down her back, over her hips, to massage the round flesh of her buttocks. He pushed her pelvis forward, thrusting her feminine delta against his bulging arousal.

He released her mouth. His lips seared the side of her face and neck, his tongue tasting the sweet womanly essence that was Rebecca Jane. "I can't be gentle, baby. I want you too badly. Forgive me."

His big hands fumbled with the release of her bra, breaking the fragile catch in his impatience. The cool evening air hit her damp flesh, tightening her already pouting nipples to aching erection. She wanted him to touch her. When he did, she cried out with excruciating pleasure-pain. He cupped her breasts, the pads of his thumbs circling the tips.

"Oh, Quent! It's too much." She tried to draw away from him, but he held her breasts, squeezing them.

Her knees buckled and only the strength in his arm going around her waist kept her on her feet. He lowered his head and took one begging nipple into his mouth. Beck moaned, the sound a keen female reaction. Her body trembled as his mouth performed magic, suckling her, bringing the ache to an unbearable point. Sexual pressure built in the womanly apex between her thighs, throbbing, pleading for satisfaction. Quent slipped his hand inside the back of her panties, gripped the waistband and tugged them downward. Beck wiggled, helping him remove her one remaining garment.

"Do you have any idea how bad I want you?" He spread one hand across the curve above her hips and drew her closer, her sensitized breasts glorying in the feel of his hairy chest. His other hand massaged the tender flesh of her soft, downy mound.

The ache inside her grew, the secret parts of her body tightening and releasing, rehearsing for the act of abandon yet to come. "I've never wanted a man the way I want you. I've never known what it was to hurt with need."

He delved inside her wet, welcoming warmth.

"You're so hot...so wet...so ready." He plunged his tantalizing fingers in and out, the movement placing pressure where she was already sensitive. When she cried out, he swallowed the sound as his tongue invaded her mouth.

She clung to him, her hands moving wildly over his shoulders and back. When he let her come up for air, she buried her face against the muscular hardness of his shoulder, her tongue tasting the salty tips of his curly body hair. "Please, Quent, don't make me wait."

Quickly he unzipped his jeans and pulled them and his briefs down his long, hairy legs, then kicked them across the floor. For one split second he thought about taking her into the bedroom, but doubted he could make it that far. His arousal was hard and tight and demanded immediate attention.

With his tongue ravishing the inside of her mouth, Quent walked Beck backward until she encountered the couch. He eased her down then remained poised above her, his sheer size enough to intimidate the woman beneath him.

Beck looked up at the big man braced above her, his hands balanced on each side of her. His face was covered in moisture, a combination of rain and sweat. The veins in his neck visibly throbbed, and the muscles in his chest flexed. Her gaze moved to the rip cord leanness of his stomach and lower to his pulsating need. Mindless with a desire beyond her control, she reached out and ran her fingernails down his chest, across his stomach and over his manhood.

"You need it slow and sweet, baby, but I can't..." His fingers massaged the nub of her passion. She moaned. With one swift, sure thrust, he entered her and her cry of acceptance rang in his ears like a seductive love song, far more erotic than the hot, syrupy saxophone music playing in the background.

He cried out, then remained perfectly still for an endless moment of rapture, a feeling beyond any explanation filled him. "You're so hot, so tight..." he groaned as she writhed beneath him, her body fitting itself snugly to the width and breadth of his arousal. "Take me," he said, filling her completely.

"I feel...I feel..." She arched upward, seeking and finding a closer fit, taking all of him, knowing that their bodies had been created for this moment, this perfect union of softness and hardness. "I feel so full."

His mouth covered her breast, sucking, licking. "I want to stay inside you forever." But even as he uttered the words, his body gave notice that it was reaching the pinnacle.

"Oh, Quent, what's happening?" The pressure had built until it demanded release. She could feel the wildness. She was reaching, reaching, the urgency growing and growing, expanding until it burst, flooding her body with ecstasy. Warmth spread out from her center, heated, prickly sensations tingling through her body as the force of her climax claimed her, and she clung to Quent, loving him in every way a woman can love a man.

"So good..." He clenched his teeth, straining, trying to hold back the inevitable storm consuming him. He wanted to make it last longer, but once Beck climaxed, he lost control. Grabbing her hips, he urged her higher and higher against him, while her body convulsed around him, the shudders of her release shattering the last remnants of his control. And he was lost to the ultimate pleasure, surrendering triumphantly.

"I love you," she whispered, her sated body still quivering with the aftershocks of such wild, untamed loving.

It had never been like this before. Never. And he knew that it could never be this good with another woman. Only with Beck. "You're everything, everything I ever wanted," he said, burrowing into the couch, pulling her to his side and then moving her so that she lay partly on the couch and partly on top of him.

Their sweat-glistened bodies lay entwined, her soft warm flesh merging with his hair-roughened hot skin. Beck closed her eyes, savoring the incredible new feeling, and wondered how she could have lived so long without knowing such perfect fulfillment. Nothing had ever been like this before, and nothing ever would again, except with Quent.

The spectacular thunder-and-lightning show had long since ended, leaving only the slow, steady rain that had set in for the night. Clad in her red silk dressing gown and nothing else, Beck stood at the bedroom windows watching and listening to the rain while she sipped a glass of white wine. The tape Quent had just put in the stereo began to play.

He entered the room, dressed casually in his loosely belted blue robe that hung open in front, creating a vee from neck to navel. He carried a tray of cheese and Melba toast.

"Like my musical selection?" he asked, placing the tray on the nightstand.

"George Shearing." The song was "Her," and as Beck turned to face Quent, the sweet violin music danced around her while the seductive ripeness of the saxophone's unique resonance caressed every newly awakened nerve in her body.

He saw the hunger in her eyes, that renewed desire to be taken to the heights and dropped to free-fall into paradise.

"Dance with me." He took a step toward her and held out his arms.

She slipped into his embrace, their bodies merging into one. Looking into his eyes, she saw a reflection of her own longing, and she smiled. One melody ended and another began. " 'Here's That Rainy Day,' " she said. "Appropriate tune, don't you think?"

"I'm not thinking," he told her, insinuating his knee between her legs as he moved her slowly to the music. "I'm just feeling."

"What are you feeling?" she asked breathlessly, her fingers creeping up the back of his neck and threading through his thick brown hair.

He pulled her against his arousal. "What are *you* feeling?" He kissed her neck just above her collarbone while his nose nudged her dressing gown apart.

"I feel empty," she said as she untied his belt and let it fall to the floor.

His big hands bunched her gown up about her hips, then slipped beneath to caress the back of her thighs and rounded behind. "This time I'm not in a hurry. I want to make it last all night."

"So do I." She met his lips in a kiss so mutually tender, so breathtakingly loving that she gave herself to him willingly when he lifted her into his arms and placed her on the bed.

He opened her dressing gown and exposed her naked body, pink and sweetly scented from their recent shower. His hands moved over her in slow, easy exploration. Beck luxuriated in the feel, her insides tightening, preparing for the culmination of their gradually growing passion. She wanted this man and this one perfect night with him. Regardless of what tomorrow and the days and weeks that followed would bring into their lives, tonight belonged to them and nothing could ever take it away.

From the moment they'd met, she'd known on some instinctive level that Quent Yerby was her destiny and there was no escaping the inevitable. She loved him, loved him with a passion she'd only read about in romantic novels. But did they have a future? If they caught Royce Paxton and put him away forever, could they build a life for themselves and Josh?

Although she'd learned to trust Quent's strength, she couldn't completely erase her unease. He was such a physical man, a man whose past and possible future reeked of violence. The man she loved, the man in whose arms she lay, had killed, and if he ever returned to the police force, he might have to kill again.

His hands covered her breasts, gently squeezing, tenderly rotating the palms over her sensitive nipples. Suddenly she forgot all her anxieties, all her concerns about tomorrow. "You're so hard," she whispered.

"You're not playing fair," he said. "If you keep doing that, I won't last another minute, let alone all night."

She laughed, slid her hand up and down his length, then released him. "Slow and easy this time."

"Fast and furious next time."

God, would he ever get enough of her? he wondered. It had been years since he'd wanted any woman so much. Just the sight of her, the smell and touch of her was enough to drive him insane. He'd taken her once in a fury so rough that, afterward, he'd been afraid he'd hurt her, but she assured him that their first mating had been as earth-shatteringly wonderful for her as for him. Tonight was theirs. They both understood the importance of what they were experiencing. She'd even said the words, and he wondered if she felt cheated that he had not returned them.

He loved her, there was no doubt about it, but he was afraid to tell her. She was no ordinary woman, not his Rebecca Jane. She was special, and far too good for the likes of him. Reluctantly he admitted that he felt a bit inferior to his lover, a lady with money and class and a doctorate degree. Compared to her, he was just a two-bit ex-cop, a man whose life was prone to violence. Even if they did love each other and wanted to give Josh a real family, would a union between two people so different have a chance?

"Let's do it all," she said. "Everything. Teach me everything." Beck found his tiny nipples hidden beneath curling chest chairs. Her tongue laved one and then the other, and she cherished the sound of his guttural moans.

"Come here," he growled as he lifted her hips and surged into her.

"Quent!" The feel of him inside her was indescribably delicious.

Their joining was the purest, simplest form of mating. Hard, demanding male imbedded within soft, nurturing female. Her emptiness filled by him. His animalistic ache soothed by her sheathing body. Her feminine longing brought to fulfillment by his masculine power. Together they became one strong, surging entity. By giving themselves over to the natural elements of their sexes, they became equals in a way two people can when their hearts and souls have mated as surely as their bodies.

Ten

Beck watched Quent strap on the shoulder holster, check his gun and insert it into the leather sheath. Her heart beat erratically, the roar filling her head, deafening her to his words.

Realizing Beck wasn't listening to him, Quent took her by the shoulders and shook her gently. "It'll be all right. Captain Burgess has posted a man at both entrances downstairs."

"If you think this is a setup, then why go?" Beck asked, eagerly moving into Quent's open arms.

He enclosed her in his embrace, pulling her against him, savoring her sweet smell and the warm, comforting feel of her body. "If there's a chance this guy who called the station knows where Paxton is, we can't just ignore him. We have to follow up on every lead."

Beck snuggled her head against Quent's shoulder. "I know. It's just that nothing we've done this past week has drawn Paxton out. It's as if he knows we've been setting traps for him."

"You think this time he's setting a trap for us?"

She pulled away from him and began pacing about the living room. "God, I don't know." She covered her eyes with her hands and breathed in and out. "I don't like the idea of your playing policeman. You enjoy it too much."

"Beck—" He reached out for her but was thwarted by her hands brushing him aside.

"Don't try to deny it. I've been living with you day and night this whole week. I've seen the look in your eyes, the excitement in your voice. You love the whole damn sordid, violent—"

He took hold of her shoulders and whirled her around to face him. "That's where you're wrong! I don't love the violence, but I do love seeing criminals brought in from the streets. I love knowing that a killer will be put away where he belongs so he won't be free to kill again."

She sobbed as she threw her arms around his neck and drew him to her. "I'm sorry. I'm so sorry. I should never have said such a thing. I know the kind of man you are, but..."

"We'll work through this, Beck." He kissed the teardrops moistening her cheekbone.

"I know you have to go now." She looked up at him, hoping only love showed, that none of the fear and uncertainties were evident.

Quent kissed her, long and hard, as if he thought this might be the last kiss they'd ever share. She clung to him, afraid to let him go.

He pushed her away, and she could see the regret in his eyes. "I'll be okay," she said.

"I'll be back as soon as I can." He walked out the door, not once looking back.

The minute the door slammed shut, Beck slumped down into a nearby chair. She knew she could never live as a policeman's wife, not knowing from one moment to the next if her husband was in danger. She simply didn't have the emotional makeup to live life on the edge. Loving Quent the way she did made her vulnerable.

The six days since Josh had left had been the longest days of her life. She'd thought that, by now, Royce Paxton would be in jail, and she and Quent and Josh would be free to go on with their lives. Twice Captain Burgess had set a trap for Paxton, using Beck as bait, and twice their quarry had been too smart to get caught.

Beck was fast reaching the breaking point. Her nerves were frazzled and she'd started thinking irrationally. The days seemed like some long, endless nightmare from which she couldn't awaken.

But the nights had become a fantasy, hours apart from the rest of her life. At night she was a seductive tigress being tamed by the master, and in turn she was *Woman* with the power to give *Man* the sublime pleasure. During their hours of lovemaking, there was no fear, no uncertainty and no tomorrow. Nothing existed except the hot, wild matings that temporarily sated—the crescendo loving that climaxed in a mad frenzy.

The phone rang. Beck jumped, then sat deadly still looking at the instrument as if it had become a living thing. Finally she forced herself to move. With trembling fingers, she picked up the receiver.

"Hello?" Her voice quivered despite her resolve to stay calm.

"Beck, it's Pete."

She let out a long sigh. "Oh. Hi, Pete."

"Just wanted to let you know that I'm closing up and heading home. I checked and there's a policeman at the front door and the back door."

"Thanks, Pete."

"You all right, Beck?"

"Just a little jumpy," she admitted. "I'm worried about Quent. If he actually encounters Paxton tonight..."

"Hey, don't worry about our Quent. He can take care of himself. He's one tough dude."

"Yes, I know." Beck hung up the phone.

Pete was right. Quent Yerby was one tough dude, and a tough dude didn't need some weepy female worrying herself silly about him.

During the next hour, Beck drank two cups of tea, listened to a Herbic Mann album, rearranged her lingerie drawer and tried to start rereading one of her favorite historical romances.

Sitting on the couch, staring at a page that had blurred in front of her eyes, Beck didn't expect the knock on the door. She let out a tiny, startled cry. *Get hold of yourself. Go to the door and ask who it is.*

With a churning stomach and weak knees, Beck walked to the door. Her shaking hand hesitated over the doorknob. "Yes, who's there?"

"It's Officer Reilly, Dr. Kendrick," the voice on the other side of the door replied. "Captain Burgess just contacted us. It seems the informant was a ruse to get Lieutenant Yerby away from here. Paxton has been spotted nearby."

A hot, searing surge of fear raced through Beck as she unlocked and opened the door. "Oh, no!"

The tall slender young officer stepped inside. He was clean-shaven and well-groomed, with short dark hair and wire-framed glasses. "There's nothing to worry about, Dr. Kendrick. Captain Burgess and Lieutenant Yerby are on their way here right now. They wanted me to come up and stay with you until they get here."

"Yes, of course. Please come in and sit down." Beck turned back toward the living room.

"Yes ma'am. Thank you." He followed her, but didn't sit down. "You might want to go check on the boy, just in case my knocking woke him up."

"What?" At first his statement didn't quite register in Beck's mind.

"If you'd like, I can go with you to check on him and reassure him that everything's okay." The young officer smiled.

Like blood oozing slowly from an open wound, realization seeped into Beck's consciousness. If this young man thought Josh was asleep in the bedroom, he wasn't one of the policemen posted downstairs to guard her.

"No, it's all right. If... if Josh was awake, he'd call for me." Beck looked, really looked at the smiling young man. She tried not to stare, but she made a quick study of his face. Paxton. She'd opened the door and let Royce Paxton walk in.

"I think you'd feel better if you checked on him," Paxton said. "I'll go with you."

"You're right." How was she going to get away from him? she wondered. How long would he wait before killing her? "The bedroom's this way."

Beck led him inside Quent and Josh's bedroom and, without flipping on a light, walked over to one of the empty beds. Paxton followed, and when he was directly beside Beck, he pulled out his gun and shot toward the bed. Instinctively, without thinking, Beck screamed. Paxton moved closer to the bed and began tearing apart the covers.

Beck crept backward, easing her way toward the door. Suddenly he whirled around. "He's not here. Where is he?"

Beck froze to the spot, her eyes riveted to the gun in Paxton's hand. "He's in a place where you'll never find him."

"I'll find him, but first I'll take care of you." He aimed the gun.

Beck dashed through the door into the living room just as Paxton fired. The bullet barely missed her.

"Go ahead and run, bitch. I'll catch you."

Beck ran through the open front door, her heart thundering in her ears, adrenaline coursing in her veins like liquid fire. Where were the two guards? Why hadn't they stopped Paxton?

She fled down the stairs, Paxton close behind her. In the dark, eerie stillness she could hear him breathing. Then she heard the earsplitting sound of his gun firing again. She dropped to her knees, knowing he couldn't see her in the darkness of the stairwell and would think she was still standing.

"Yerby will never get back here in time to save you," Paxton taunted. "He's off on a wild goose chase."

Beck crawled down the remaining three steps to the back hallway. Trying to control her hysterical breathing, she put her hand in her mouth and bit down hard. The self-inflicted pain calmed her.

She had to get out of The Jungle, but how? It was black as pitch down here. Obviously Paxton had turned off all the lights. But she didn't dare turn one on and show him her location.

The back door! It was close. She could feel her way.

Edging slowly along the wall, Beck saw a dim light coming through the back door. Just a shadowy reflection from the streetlight shining into the alley, but enough light to guide her to the nearest escape route. Staying close to the wall, Beck moved toward her destination.

But Paxton was gaining on her. She could hear him. She could feel him closing in on her. *Hurry...Hurry!* her mind screamed. Just a few more feet to the back door.

Her feet encountered an obstacle right in front of the door. Losing her balance as she stumbled over the massive lump, Beck fell to her knees, landing on top of a human body. She cried out before her brain could issue a warning not to.

"I see you've found Officer Reilly." Paxton stood over her.

She couldn't see his face, only the shadowy reflection of his lanky body. She wasn't going to die like this. Not without a fight. Beck rose, her hand grabbing for Paxton's arm. When he reached back to slap her away, she stood up quickly and took him off guard, her shoulder ramming into his hand. The clatter of his gun as it hit the floor echoed in her ears.

"I don't need a gun to kill you." His voice sounded the way it had that day in the parking deck—sinisterly happy.

He struck her across the shoulder. Beck swayed backward, but caught herself against the wall. She knew he was going to strike again, knew he would enjoy killing her slowly the way he had Jill. She had to get away from him. But how? If only she'd taken those self-defense lessons with Keela. Hit him in the groin, she could hear her secretary saying when she'd told Beck about the classes.

Paxton's huge fist found its mark in the darkness. Beck groaned with pain when his knuckles punched into her stomach. No, no, he wasn't going to beat her. No one would ever beat her again. Quent had promised. He'd promised he'd never let anyone hurt her. With a strength born of fear and rage, Beck brought her knee up and blindly thrust into her attacker's body.

Paxton's earsplitting yell told her that her shot in the dark had hit home. While he rolled off a string of obscenities, Beck darted past him and down the long hallway. Escape! She had to escape. Intending to head toward the front of the building, Beck became confused in the darkness and turned into an interior room. Realizing her mistake, she tried to close the door behind her, but Paxton was there, pushing, forcing it open.

Bending to his superior strength, Beck released the door and flattened her back against the wall. Paxton flew into the room. She could hear him breathing, see the outline of his body silhouetted against the opaque windows lining one outside wall. She took a deep, calming breath, and the smell of chlorine filled her nostrils.

Muted light from the world on Overton Square passed through the glass wall into the pool area.

"Can you swim?" Paxton asked.

"It's Reilly. He's dead. Bullet in his head just like Humphrey's out front. Damn, what kind of maniac are we dealing with?" Captain Burgess knelt down beside the handsome young officer who would never reach his twenty-fifth birthday.

"I should have known better." Quent stepped around Burgess. "My gut instincts told me Paxton was setting us up. If he's hurt her—"

"Get hold of yourself. Losing it won't help Dr. Kendrick." Burgess stood up. "I've got men posted all around the building."

"I want Paxton. Do you hear me?' Quent turned to face his former commanding officer. The scant light from the alley poured through the open door and cast dim shadows over several feet of the hallway.

"Let my men check the place out. You don't even know if they're still here. He could have taken her anywhere."

"She's here. I can feel it," Quent said. "Go get your sharpshooters, but keep them behind me. Understand?"

"Quent?"

"He's mine," Quent said, and pulled his 9 mm automatic from the holster.

Quent's foot encountered a small object on the floor. He bent over and picked it up.

"A gun?" Burgess asked.

"Probably Paxton's."

"That means he's unarmed."

Quent leaned back against the wall, perspiration dotting his forehead. Hesitating for a split second, he returned his own gun to the holster.

"We'll back you up," Burgess said.

Quent heard Beck's shrill scream and then the sound of splashing water. "The pool!"

"Wait, you damned fool," Burgess said, his voice just above a whisper.

Unheeding any orders from Burgess or his own trained mind, Quent ran headlong toward the sound of Beck's cries. *God, don't let me be too late,* he prayed.

Paxton pulled Beck out of the pool, placing her wet body between his outstretched legs. His long, slender fingers circled her throat as he bent over her. "The last thing you're going to remember is my hands all over your body."

White hot rage engulfed Quent as he ran into the room and lunged for the man threatening Beck. The force of Quent's big body slamming into him knocked Paxton on top of Beck. Quent slugged his opponent in the jaw. The two men, locked in combat, rolled around on the tile floor. Beck struggled to her feet and stood helplessly while Quent and Paxton fought.

In the semidarkness she could distinguish one man from the other only by Quent's larger frame. Suddenly a shiny metal object appeared in Paxton's hand, and Beck realized he'd pulled out a knife. "Quent, he's got a knife," she yelled as she ran toward the two men.

But Quent already knew. Paxton had slashed Quent's chest, and blood was seeping through the tears in his shirt. Momentarily stunned by the unexpected assault, Quent lost his hold on the other man.

Paxton reached out and grabbed Beck around the neck. "Stay where you are, Yerby, or I'll gut her like a hog."

Beck felt the cold steel edge pressing against her stomach. Bile rose in her throat. "Quent."

"Let her go, Paxton. You're a dead man if you hurt her," Quent said. Where were Burgess and his sharpshooters? he wondered. They'd damn well better hurry.

"I'm leaving here in one piece," Paxton said, edging backward, away from Quent.

Beck didn't struggle, knowing one false move on her part could prompt her assailant into deadly action. She wondered how far from the pool they were. If only Paxton would move closer, she might be able to trip him and land them both in the water. At least that way she'd have a chance of getting away.

"Let her go, and we'll talk." Quent took a tentative step forward.

"Stay right where you are, Yerby." Paxton eased backward, pulling Beck with him. "I thought I'd have more time with our beautiful Dr. Kendrick. I figured I'd be finished with her long before you realized what was going on."

"You figured wrong," Quent said, taking one more step forward.

"Don't try it," Paxton said, and pulled Beck to his side, placing the knife at her throat. "She wouldn't be of much use to you with her throat slit."

Beck felt the side of the pool beneath her foot. With her body held tightly against Paxton's side, she had little ability to maneuver. She eased her foot farther toward the pool, dangling it over the side of the smooth tile until the tip of her shoe touched the water. Knowing she'd have only one chance to unbalance her attacker, Beck leaned all her weight against Paxton, forcing him backward.

"What the—" Paxton lost his footing and swayed, his body falling down, down, down. He clutched at thin air, and the arm restraining Beck dropped away just as they hit the water.

Warm, chlorinated liquid engulfed Beck, and she struggled to surface. Paxton, dazed by her unexpected move, fought against the pressure of the water surrounding him.

"Swim away from him," Quent yelled.

Beck looked up to see Quent standing at the pool's edge. He held something in his hands. His gun! "Don't!" she cried.

Quent's hands were steady, his aim sure. All he had to do was pull the trigger. He'd never wanted to see a man dead as badly as he did Paxton. The very thought of what he'd put Beck and Josh through was enough to warrant the man's execution. It would be so simple. So easy. He wanted to pull the trigger. He wanted to kill.

Suddenly Captain Burgess stormed into the room. The SWAT team followed him and surrounded the pool.

"Help Dr. Kendrick out of the pool," Burgess said. "Our boy Paxton isn't going to do a thing but wait for us to drag him out."

Quent held the 9 mm tightly in his big hands, hands that weren't so steady now. The urge to eliminate a vicious animal like Paxton held Quent hostage to his own violent emotions.

"Please, Quent." Beck swam to the edge of the pool and reached out for Quent's assistance. "Help me."

He took his eyes off Paxton for a split second to look at Beck. Although his eyes had adjusted to the semidarkness of the room, he couldn't make out the expression on her face. All he could see was one outstretched hand.

Quent released his tenacious hold on his gun, stood up straight and returned the automatic to the holster. Moving quickly, he reached the pool's edge, grabbed Beck and pulled her up into his arms.

She stood there, soaking wet and trembling, while he ran his hands over her body as if needing to reassure himself that she was unharmed. He released her, took her damp face in both hands and just looked at her.

"Sweet thing," he said. "My sweet thing."

Those were the most precious words Beck had ever heard, that damned annoying little endearment Quent used for three-fourths of the female population. With tears in her eyes, Beck laughed and threw her arms around his neck.

Captain Burgess patted Quent on the back. "We can handle things from here. Why don't you take Dr. Kendrick upstairs? We can tie up any loose ends tomorrow."

Quent held Beck while they watched two policemen pull Paxton from the pool. Compliant, easily managed, almost docile, Jill's killer allowed the officers to read him his rights and handcuff him.

"Why didn't you kill me, Yerby?" Paxton asked. "She made you weak. They do that to a man if you don't keep 'em in line."

Beck felt Quent tense, every muscle in his body tightened. She clung to him, her fingers gripping his jacket. When she moved her hand upward, she encountered the bulge of his shoulder holster. She trembled.

"Get him out of here," Captain Burgess said.

As the policemen escorted him out of the room, Paxton called out, "You wanted to shoot me, but you couldn't. You were too afraid of what she'd think about you. That's why I won, why I'm stronger. No woman ever made me weak."

Beck wondered what Quent was thinking as they watched Paxton being taken away. Did Quent regret not shooting Royce Paxton when he had the chance? She wanted to tell him that she was so proud of him and loved him all the more for resisting the urge to kill.

"He's wrong, you know," she said, laying her head on Quent's shoulder as he circled her waist with his arm. "You aren't weak. You're the strongest, bravest, most—"

He whirled her around into his arms and covered her mouth with his own. The kiss silenced her as it claimed her.

When he ended the kiss, he placed his open palm at her neck and ran his thumb and fingers up and down, stroking her damp flesh. "Yeah, he was wrong about a lot of things. You're my weakness, all right, but you don't make me weak. You make me strong, strong in ways I never knew mattered."

She loved him at that moment more than she ever thought possible. The nightmare had ended. They had survived. All that lay ahead now was the future. Their future.

Eleven

"I don't want to talk," Quent said. "I don't need to evaluate my feelings or come to terms with what happened tonight."

"You can't keep it bottled up inside you." Beck ran a comb through her long, damp hair as she sat at her dressing table.

"Dammit, do you have to sound so much like a psychologist?"

"I *am* a psychologist." Beck laid down the comb and turned around to where she could face Quent. "And I think that bothers you."

"You could have died tonight, and here you are cool as a cucumber and ready to play psychoanalyst." He stood in the middle of her bedroom, big and overpowering in his rage.

"You're angry about what happened tonight. Because you weren't in control all the time. You think you let me down."

"Do you know how close you came to dying?"

"That wasn't your fault." She stood up and walked over to him. "I didn't die. I'm alive and well." She slipped her hand inside his unbuttoned shirt and ran her fingertips across the bandaged knife cuts on his chest. "You're the one who got hurt."

"Scratches," he said, with typical male bravado.

She smiled. "Yeah, scratches."

"I wanted to kill him." Quent searched her face for a reaction to his words.

"I know." Her voice was as soft and tender as an evening breeze. "But you didn't." She touched his face, the lightest, most delicate touch imaginable.

He grabbed her by the shoulders and squeezed. "I've never felt so helpless. All I could think was that if I lost you, I lost everything."

She closed her eyes against the torment she saw on his face, and she knew, whether he said the words or not, that he loved her. And that love was as strong and powerful as the love she felt for him. But would love be enough? Now that she and Josh were safe, could she and Quent build a life together?

"We can put that behind us," Beck told him. "We have to think about the future, about giving Josh a normal, secure life. You and I—"

"By God, if you tell me that we're too different to ever make a go of things..." He tightened his hold on her slender shoulders.

"Before we met, our life-styles were quite different. We have some difficult decisions to make. We have to think things through carefully."

"I don't want to think. Not tonight. Not now."

She couldn't stop herself from staring at him, at his hard, lean face and those incredible blue eyes. The hunger she saw there both frightened and exhilarated her.

"What do you see?" he asked.

"You want me." She felt the heat rising through her. Born in the depths of her femininity, it grew warmer and brighter as it spread to every nerve ending in her body.

"It's that obvious, isn't it?"

"Sex won't solve all our problems." Her voice sounded raspy, even to her.

"To hell with our problems." His gaze moved over her slowly, appreciatively. He slid his hands down her back, clasping her waist and drawing her to him.

"Quent?"

"I want you squirming, panting, begging." Less than two hours ago he'd wanted her alive. Now, all he could think about was making love to her. That desperate need was linked with the fact he'd come so close to losing her.

She leaned against him, her heart beating wildly, her mind absorbing the sensuality of his words as they created a wanton image.

Her lips parted, pleading for a repeat performance of the carnal delights his mouth and tongue had taught her.

"We'll think tomorrow. We'll face our problems then." He swung her up into his arms and burrowed his face into her throat. She smelled of that fancy perfume she always wore, that exotic flowery scent.

He laid her down on the bed, hovering over her just long enough to shed his clean shirt. With gentle fingers he untied the belt of her red dressing gown and spread the garment open. When he reached out and touched her parted lips, she sighed and closed her eyes.

"Take it off," he told her.

She opened her eyes when she heard the commanding tone of his voice, and watched while he removed the rest of his clothing. Obediently she rose off the bed enough to slip out of her dressing gown.

With swift intent, he came down on her, his lips capturing hers as his big body covered her slender frame. Mindless with the hunger building inside her, Beck clutched his massive shoulders as his tongue invaded the softness of her mouth.

She wanted to slow the tempest raging inside her, but his hands were moving over her, stroking her, tormenting her. Tonight won't be enough, she wanted to cry, but all she could do was respond to his touch, to the insistent pull of desire in the apex between her thighs. Why couldn't she resist this purely physical magic between them? And then she knew. It wasn't just a physical thing for her. It was so much more. If only it were for him, too.

"You want me," he said, his mouth near her breast. "Tell me. Let me hear you say it."

He nipped at her breast, then loved it with his tongue. She squirmed beneath him. "Yes, I want you. I want you so much."

His lips moved on a downward path, seeking and finding every vulnerable inch of her naked flesh. He coated her outer thigh with moisture and made his way back up her inner thigh, his tongue and teeth taking turns.

Her body became one huge sensation, pure female action and reaction as her own hands went into play, roaming his shoulders and back and buttocks.

Suddenly she found herself hoisted off the bed and over on top of Quent. She lay there, stunned, as her legs straddled his hips.

"You do it, baby," he said, taking her hands in his and bringing them down to his arousal.

Her lips curled into a smile. He had put her in charge, given her the power, the dominant position. Her hand encircled his hardness, and she listened to his groans with great satisfaction. This big, virile man was as much within her control as she was his.

With a quick sure move, she rose over him and buried him deep within her. Her breathing quickened to sharp little pants and she moaned, throwing her head back and clenching his shoulders. Her fingernails bit into his muscles.

Quent clutched her hips and together they began their ride of passion. She watched as their bodies moved in perfect rhythm, and he watched her, the way her high, round breasts swayed above his mouth, the way her face tightened with pleasure as he surged into her.

He took one nipple into his mouth and sucked greedily. She inhaled her cry of joyous agony. When his tongue played with her breast, pressing against her, covering the tip with such hot dampness, Beck thought she'd lose her mind. The feeling was so intense she wasn't sure she could bear any more.

Her body clenched him, tightened and relaxed as it sought that one perfect moment of bliss. He released her breast long enough to whisper, "Faster. Slower. Anyway you want it, baby. You can make it happen."

"Faster," she cried out. "Harder and faster."

He arched up and she accelerated the speed of her ride. They moved in a frenzy of desire until his face contorted in spasms of release. The moment she felt his climax, Beck reached higher and higher until ecstasy burst within her, and she fell headlong into oblivion, that deep, warm, sated oblivion.

He held her on top of him until their heartbeats returned to a more normal speed and her lips sought his. He knew he'd acted like an untamed animal, and had brought out the primitive instincts in her. She'd given. He'd taken. And in those final seconds of his possession, she claimed him body and soul. He was hers. If Rebecca Jane Kendrick hadn't walked into his life two months ago, he never would have known the wonder of love.

Beck eased her sweat-dampened body off his and rolled over to lie beside him. He slipped his arm around her and she snuggled close. They kissed. And one kiss led to another and another.

"Quent?"

"Huh?"

"Call me sweet thing."

He laughed and tightened his arms around her. "My sweet thing," he whispered, his lips against her ear. *"Mine."*

In the dark, still hours of early morning they made love again. And though his loving contained an element of wildness, there was no brutality in Quent Yerby.

Beck pulled her hair back into a loose ponytail and tied it with a red ribbon. She gave herself a quick once-over in the mirror, turned and, bracing herself, went into the living room. Quent sat on the couch, one long leg crossed straight over the other. When Beck entered the room, he threw down the newspaper in his hand and stood up.

"You look wonderful," he said, that crooked, cocky little grin on his face.

Beck returned his smile, a faint warm blush creeping into her cheeks. "I feel pretty wonderful." After spending the night in Quent's arms and sharing the satisfaction of their loving more than once, she felt complete and fulfilled and almost giddy.

"There's hot coffee and tea in the kitchen." He wanted to reach out and take her in his arms, but knew that now was not the time. If he touched her, they'd be making love within a few minutes. This morning was reality time. Last night they had postponed thinking and talking about the future. Today, with Josh on his way home, decisions could no longer be delayed.

"Maybe later." She sat down in a chair beside the couch.

"D day, huh?" He sat back down on the couch and faced her.

"Elise said eleven. They should be here anytime now." Beck clutched her hands in her lap and leaned back in the chair. "Oh, Quent, didn't Josh sound happy? I was so afraid this separation would do some irreparable damage."

"Hey, he's a Yerby. We're a tough bunch."

"You're right." Beck looked down at her hands, hesitating before starting the discussion that would decide her future. "We have to talk. We have to make some decisions."

Quent shook his head affirmatively, slid his big body to the edge of the couch and let his hands dangle between his outstretched thighs. "I know a classy da—lady like you could have any guy she wanted."

"Quent—"

He threw up his hand as a stop signal. "Just let me say what I have to say."

"Go ahead."

"At first I didn't think we had anything in common except Josh. I don't have your education, your polish, your style. I'm a roughneck jock who's used his fists as much as his brains." Quent looked at her, trying to gauge her reaction. She sat, unmoving, her soft brown eyes focused on him, and her beautiful face revealing none of what she was feeling. "As a policeman I've been forced to kill a couple of times."

"You don't have to explain how violent your past has been," Beck said, taking a deep breath. "I know the kind of man you are, Quent Yerby. I've lived with you, made love with you."

"I would never hurt you. I don't like violence. I hate it. As a policeman I worked hard to get criminals off the streets, to make life safer for the people of Memphis."

"I know," she whispered, leaning over to touch his hand. "You're a protector. The only real violence in your nature is in your desire to take care of others."

"I'm capable of killing another human being. I've done it in the line of duty. I came very close to killing Paxton last night. If he'd hurt you, I probably would have killed him. Can you accept a man with that kind of a flaw?"

Tears filled her eyes, and only by willing herself to remain calm did Beck check their downward flow. "I've learned a valuable lesson from you about men."

He stared at her, seeing the light of discovery in her eyes. "What?"

"I thought all big, virile men tended to be brutal in their dealings with women. Intellectually I knew it wasn't true, but emotionally I was never able to overcome my father's abuse." She took both his big hands in her smaller ones and squeezed tightly. "You've taught me the difference between masculine strength and brutality. You're a man who could and would do violent things in order to protect others, but you would never turn that violence on those you love, on anyone weaker than you."

A lump formed in Quent's throat. He clenched his teeth to stem the tide of emotions coming to the surface. Taking Beck by her elbows, he pulled her up and guided her to the couch. She went willingly, seating herself beside him. "I'm not going back to the force. I've decided that a family man, a guy with a kid, should be in a safer line of work."

"Like owning and managing a health club?"

"Yeah. Who knows—maybe we'll be so successful I'll build The Jungle II and III. A guy could get rich."

Beck wasn't sure what he was trying to tell her. He considered himself a family man, but that could be because of Josh. Was he hinting at marriage? Was he willing to take the plunge a second time in order to give Josh a stable home life? "Josh and I will be moving back to my town house."

"That's a good idea." Quent put his arm around her shoulder and drew her back into the softness of the couch. "I love this neighborhood, but I can see the advantages for Josh growing up in Germantown."

"Does that mean you're going to allow me to adopt Josh?" She wanted to be Josh's mother legally, but somehow, that wasn't enough. She wanted more. She wanted Quent to be a part of her new family, not just a weekend father.

"There's no need for us to fight over Josh. He needs us both, and we both love and need him." He was more than willing to share his nephew with Beck. The kid needed two parents, didn't he? Hell, he could ask Beck to marry him and she'd probably say yes, but would it work out between them in the long run if they married for Josh's sake? Oh, right now, Beck saw him as a knight in shining armor—something he definitely wasn't. So, did she love him, as she'd proclaimed during the passionate hours they'd shared last night, or was she infatuated with the ideal of a future for the three of them?

"I agree." Beck sucked in her breath, straightened her shoulders and turned to Quent. She looked him squarely in the eye. "You can be irritating and impossible at times. Your manners are atrocious, and one of the few things you have good taste in is music."

When he loosed his hold about her shoulders, Beck moved to the edge of the couch and stuck her finger out, pointing it at Quent. "I know all your good qualities and all your bad ones. You are far from perfect, and not exactly the kind of man I ever thought I'd fall in love with, but I did." Beck lifted her head high. "There, I've said it. I love you, you big macho man!"

Quent's cocky, self-assured grin curled his lips. "You love me, huh? Despite the fact that I'm a crude, nonintellectual jock who'd rather spend an evening making wild crazy love to you on the floor than wining and dining you in some fancy restaurant?"

"Yes." She didn't let his amused stare fluster her composure in the least.

"Life with me will be hot dogs and doughnuts, not fillet mignon and chocolate mousse."

"We can discuss menus later."

"I'll be jealous and possessive and expect you to coddle my male ego."

"I'll be just as jealous and possessive and demand equal coddling," she said.

"We could provide Josh with a stable family and the two of us live separately..."

"Yes, we could."

"I'll want more kids," he gripped her chin in his hand. "Two."

"That's a reasonable request, but I'm thirty-four, so we should get started as soon as possible." She leaned toward him, her face alight with the joy bursting inside her.

"Ah, sweet thing, I love you," he said just before his lips covered hers with a claim of ownership.

Beck ended the kiss and pulled slightly away from him. "Say that again."

"Say that I love you?" he asked, a teasing glint in his eyes.

"Why has it taken you so long to tell me?"

"Because I was afraid of being hurt," he admitted. "You know that male ego I'm expecting you to coddle? Well, it got pretty badly crushed when I was married to Shannon. I guess I couldn't believe you really loved me. A guy like me just doesn't get that lucky."

"Oh, yes he does. Besides, I'm feeling pretty lucky myself. You're quite a catch, Mr. Yerby. I happen to know half the female population of Memphis thinks you're a *hunk*."

"I don't give a damn what half the female population of Memphis thinks. The only opinion that matters is yours." He ran a line of gentle kisses along her jawline.

Beck twined her arms around his neck and rubbed his nose with hers. "I think you're a hunk, with the most beautiful blue eyes I've ever seen."

Quent laughed and drew her to him. "Will you marry me, Rebecca Jane? Will you give me babies? Will you be my lifelong mate and grow old with me?"

The front door swung open and Josh flew into the room, a smiling Elise Zimmerman behind him.

Josh hurled himself between Quent and Beck, his little arms trying to encompass both of them. "I'm home. I'm home," he squealed. "And I don't ever have to go away again, do I?"

"He's been like this ever since I arrived at the Sellers' house," Elise said as she walked into the living room.

Beck pulled Josh onto her lap, hugging him to her, smothering him with motherly affection. "I figure the next time you leave home will be to go to college. How'll that be?"

"Where're we going to live? Are we staying here? Are we all moving back to your house?" Questions rocketed from his mouth.

Beck looked at Quent and smiled. "I think after Uncle Quent and I get married, we'll look for a house with a big backyard so we can get you a dog."

"Get married!" Elise's eyes widened in surprise. "Well, whataya know. The lady shrink and the muscle man. A match made in heaven."

Quent pulled Beck and Josh into his arms and looked over at Elise with an idiotically happy grin on his face. "No, this was a match made on Overton Square in a ratty little apartment above The Jungle.''

"Yeah," Josh said burrowing into the loving security of their arms.

Epilogue

Picnic tables laden with food covered the backyard at Holly House in Florence, Alabama. Hundreds of multicolored balloons hung from the tree limbs, floated above every chair and decorated the center of every table.

Josh Yerby sucked in his breath and released it, blowing out all six candles on his huge birthday cake.

"You get your wish," Lettie Kendrick told her younger cousin. "But you can't tell it or it won't come true."

"I already got all my wishes," the little boy said, looking across the table at his proud parents.

"Then open your presents," Lettie commanded. "I want to see if you like what me and Jeff got you."

Quent walked around the table and helped his son off the bench where he stood. The two cousins headed for a smaller table stacked high with an assortment of gift-wrapped boxes.

Lucky Kendrick picked up the husky, dark-haired toddler who was pulling on her leg and whining. "Come on, Jeff. Mommy'll get you some cake and ice cream."

Cole Kendrick held a video camera on his shoulder as he maneuvered through the bevy of youngsters flooding his backyard. "Talk while you're unwrapping your presents," Cole said. "And, Lettie, will you just sit down and watch? Josh doesn't need any help."

Quent Yerby placed an arm around his wife's shoulder and hugged her to him. "Six years old and he's already got all his wishes." Quent shook his head sadly.

"In time he'll start wishing again," Beck said. "Right now, I think Josh and I both feel as if we've gotten more than we ever thought possible."

Quent slipped one big hand down Beck's side and covered the rounded swell of her protruding stomach. "You, me, Josh and Junior, here. There's not much more I could ask for, is there? Except, maybe a little time alone with my beautiful wife later this evening."

"Well, I could make that wish come true," Beck said, looking at Quent, a seductive invitation in her eyes. "If you know the secret passwords."

He kissed her on the cheek, then moved his mouth to her ear and whispered, "I love you, sweet thing."

She giggled as she laid her head on her husband's shoulder and said, "Your wish is my command."

* * * * *

SILHOUETTE® Desire™

COMING NEXT MONTH

#667 WILD ABOUT HARRY—Linda Lael Miller
Widowed mom Amy Ryan was sure she wasn't ready to love again. But why was she simply wild about Australia's *Man of the World*, Harry Griffith?

#668 A FINE MADNESS—Kathleen Korbel
It seemed someone thought that England's *Man of the World*, Matthew Spears, and Quinn Rutledge belonged together! Could they survive an eccentric ghost's matchmaking antics and discover romance on their own?

#669 ON HIS HONOR—Lucy Gordon
When Italy's *Man of the World*, Carlo Valetti, walked back into Serena Fletcher's life, she was nervous. Was this sexy charmer there to claim *her* love—or *his* daughter?

#670 LION OF THE DESERT—Barbara Faith
Morocco's *Man of the World*, Sheik Kadim al-Raji, had a mission—to rescue Diane St. James from kidnappers. But once they were safe, would this primitive male be able to let her go?

#671 FALCONER—Jennifer Greene
Shy Leigh Merrick knew life was no fairy tale, but then she met Austria's *Man of the World*, roguish Rand Krieger. This lord of the castle sent her heart soaring....

#672 SLADE'S WOMAN—BJ James
Fragile Beth Warren never dreamed she'd ever meet anyone like America's *Man of the World*, Hunter Slade. But this solitary man just wanted to be left alone....

AVAILABLE NOW:

#661 PRIDE AND JOY
Joyce Thies

#662 OUT OF DANGER
Beverly Barton

#663 THE MIDAS TOUCH
Cathryn Clare

#664 MUSTANG VALLEY
Jackie Merritt

#665 SMOOTH SAILING
Cathie Linz

#666 LONE WOLF
Annette Broadrick

Bestselling author **NORA ROBERTS** captures all the romance, adventure, passion and excitement of Silhouette in a special miniseries.

THE CALHOUN WOMEN

Four charming, beautiful and fiercely independent sisters set out on a search for a missing family heirloom—an emerald necklace—and each finds something even more precious... passionate romance.

Look for THE CALHOUN WOMEN miniseries starting in June.

COURTING CATHERINE
in Silhouette Romance #801 (June/$2.50)

A MAN FOR AMANDA
in Silhouette Desire #649 (July/$2.75)

FOR THE LOVE OF LILAH
in Silhouette Special Edition #685 (August/$3.25)

SUZANNA'S SURRENDER
in Silhouette Intimate Moments #397 (September/$3.29)

Available at your favorite retail outlet, or order any missed titles by sending your name, address, zip code or postal code, along with a check or money order (please do not send cash) for the price shown above, plus 75¢ postage and handling ($1.00 in Canada), payable to Silhouette Reader Service to:

In the U.S.
3010 Walden Avenue
P.O. Box 1396
Buffalo, NY 14269-1396

In Canada
P.O. Box 609
Fort Erie, Ontario
L2A 5X3

Please specify book title(s) with your order.
Canadian residents add applicable federal and provincial taxes.

CALWOM-2R

Silhouette Special Edition

presents

SONNY'S GIRLS

by Emilie Richards, Celeste Hamilton and Erica Spindler

They had been Sonny's girls, irresistibly drawn to the charismatic high school football hero. Ten years later, none could forget the night that changed their lives forever.

In July—
ALL THOSE YEARS AGO by Emilie Richards (SSE #684)
Meredith Robbins had left town in shame. Could she ever banish the past and reach for love again?

In August—
DON'T LOOK BACK by Celeste Hamilton (SSE #690)
Cyndi Saint was Sonny's steady. Ten years later, she remembered only his hurtful parting words....

In September—
LONGER THAN... by Erica Spindler (SSE #696)
Bubbly Jennifer Joyce was everybody's friend. But nobody knew the secret longings she felt for bad boy Ryder Hayes....

SILHOUETTE®
OFFICIAL SWEEPSTAKES RULES

NO PURCHASE NECESSARY

1. To enter, complete an Official Entry Form or 3" × 5" index card by hand-printing, in plain block letters, your complete name, address, phone number and age, and mailing it to: Silhouette Fashion A Whole New You Sweepstakes, P.O. Box 9056, Buffalo, NY 14269-9056.

   No responsibility is assumed for lost, late or misdirected mail. Entries must be sent separately with first class postage affixed, and be received no later than December 31, 1991 for eligibility.

2. Winners will be selected by D.L. Blair, Inc., an independent judging organization whose decisions are final, in random drawings to be held on January 30, 1992 in Blair, NE at 10:00 a.m. from among all eligible entries received.

3. The prizes to be awarded and their approximate retail values are as follows: Grand Prize — A brand-new Ford Explorer 4×4 plus a trip for two (2) to Hawaii, including round-trip air transportation, six (0) nights hotel accommodation, a $1,400 meal/spending money stipend and $2,000 cash toward a new fashion wardrobe (approximate value: $28,000) or $15,000 cash; two (2) Second Prizes — A trip to Hawaii, including round-trip air transportation, six (6) nights hotel accommodation, a $1,400 meal/spending money stipend and $2,000 cash toward a new fashion wardrobe (approximate value: $11,000) or $5,000 cash; three (3) Third Prizes — $2,000 cash toward a new fashion wardrobe. All prizes are valued in U.S. currency. Travel award air transportation is from the commercial airport nearest winner's home. Travel is subject to space and accommodation availability, and must be completed by June 30, 1993. Sweepstakes offer is open to residents of the U.S. and Canada who are 21 years of age or older as of December 31, 1991, except residents of Puerto Rico, employees and immediate family members of Torstar Corp., its affiliates, subsidiaries, and all agencies, entities and persons connected with the use, marketing, or conduct of this sweepstakes. All federal, state, provincial, municipal and local laws apply. Offer void wherever prohibited by law. Taxes and/or duties, applicable registration and licensing fees, are the sole responsibility of the winners. Any litigation within the province of Quebec respecting the conduct and awarding of a prize may be submitted to the Régie des loteries et courses du Québec. All prizes will be awarded; winners will be notified by mail. No substitution of prizes is permitted.

4. Potential winners must sign and return any required Affidavit of Eligibility/Release of Liability within 30 days of notification. In the event of noncompliance within this time period, the prize may be awarded to an alternate winner. Any prize or prize notification returned as undeliverable may result in the awarding of that prize to an alternate winner. By acceptance of their prize, winners consent to use of their names, photographs or their likenesses for purposes of advertising, trade and promotion on behalf of Torstar Corp. without further compensation. Canadian winners must correctly answer a time-limited arithmetical question in order to be awarded a prize.

5. For a list of winners (available after 3/31/92), send a separate stamped, self-addressed envelope to: Silhouette Fashion A Whole New You Sweepstakes, P.O. Box 4685, Blair, NE 68009.

PREMIUM OFFER TERMS

To receive your gift, complete the Offer Certificate according to directions. Be certain to enclose the required number of "Fashion A Whole New You" proofs of product purchase (which are found on the last page of every specially marked "Fashion A Whole New You" Silhouette or Harlequin romance novel). Requests must be received no later than December 31, 1991. Limit: four (4) gifts per name, family, group, organization or address. Items depicted are for illustrative purposes only and may not be exactly as shown. Please allow 6 to 8 weeks for receipt of order. Offer good while quantities of gifts last. In the event an ordered gift is no longer available, you will receive a free, previously unpublished Silhouette or Harlequin book for every proof of purchase you have submitted with your request, plus a refund of the postage and handling charge you have included. Offer good in the U.S. and Canada only.

SLFW-SWPR

SILHOUETTE® OFFICIAL SWEEPSTAKES ENTRY FORM

4-FWSOS-2

Complete and return this Entry Form immediately – the more entries you submit, the better your chances of winning!

- Entries must be received by **December 31, 1991**.
- A Random draw will take place on **January 30, 1992**.
- No purchase necessary.

Yes, I want to win a FASHION A WHOLE NEW YOU Sensuous and Adventurous prize from Silhouette:

Name _____ Telephone _____ Age _____

Address _____

City _____ State _____ Zip _____

Return Entries to: **Silhouette FASHION A WHOLE NEW YOU,**
P.O. Box 9056, Buffalo, NY 14269-9056   © 1991 Harlequin Enterprises Limited

PREMIUM OFFER

To receive your free gift, send us the required number of proofs-of-purchase from any specially marked FASHION A WHOLE NEW YOU Silhouette or Harlequin Book with the Offer Certificate properly completed, plus a check or money order (do not send cash) to cover postage and handling payable to Silhouette FASHION A WHOLE NEW YOU Offer. We will send you the specified gift.

OFFER CERTIFICATE

Item	A. SENSUAL DESIGNER VANITY BOX COLLECTION (set of 4) (Suggested Retail Price $60.00)	B. ADVENTUROUS TRAVEL COSMETIC CASE SET (set of 3) (Suggested Retail Price $25.00)
# of proofs-of-purchase	18	12
Postage and Handling	$3.50	$2.95
Check one	☐	☐

Name _____

Address _____

City _____ State _____ Zip _____

Mail this certificate, designated number of proofs-of-purchase and check or money order for postage and handling to: **Silhouette FASHION A WHOLE NEW YOU Gift Offer, P.O. Box 9057, Buffalo, NY 14269-9057.** Requests must be received by December 31, 1991.

ONE PROOF-OF-PURCHASE

4-FWSDP-2

To collect your fabulous free gift you must include the necessary number of proofs-of-purchase with a properly completed Offer Certificate.

© 1991 Harlequin Enterprises Limited

See previous page for details.